DISAPPEARANCES

?

JOHN R. SUTHER,

AUTHOR

VERBENA, ALABAMA,

36091

Dedicated To My Lovely Wife Ruth,
And My Good Friend and Editor, Susan Putman

ISBN 10: 0615907326
13: 9780615907321

CHAPTER 1

In the dim light, Ricky Roberts noticed the
time on his wristwatch as 4:10. He said to himself,
"I'm running a few minutes late as usual."

He put the gear lever in reverse, and backed
his pickup truck slowly out of the driveway to the
street. He then put it in drive, pressed on the gas
pedal, maybe a little too hard, because the tires
spun, squealed, and away he went to Casper, a dirt
street on the edge of town.

Ricky drove down to the end of the street, to
the drive on the right, stopped, and lightly blew
his horn.

In a few minutes, the front door at the house
opened and a portly middle-aged female came out.

In her possession, she had a large purse, and when she opened the door to Ricky's pickup, threw the purse in, grunted, " Good morning " climbed in and once suitably seated, fastened her seatbelt.

Ricky knew not to move the truck until she was ready, as she would "pitch a fit", and some folks asked them why they didn't fire her, then, they tasted her cooking, and 'enough' said!

When they arrived at the restaurant, Ricky pulled around behind, then backed into the parking lot that was facing the other street. Satisfying himself that no one was lurking in the alley, they got out of the truck and entered the rear door.

A few minutes later, Pete and Marjorie Edwards entered, and after exchanging greetings, Marjorie went straight to work filling the salt, and pepper shakers. Then she told Pete to go downstairs and bring up a bag of sugar and a bundle of napkins.

"Aye, aye," answered Pete and starting out of the room stopped, and looking at Ricky, said laughingly, "Boss man, you've got to stop this slave driver, she's killing me." Later on, after the breakfast rush with was over, Rita came in, as she usually did, to help prepare the lunch menu. There were still a few tables occupied with the usual talkers.

"Good morning, all", Rita called out cheerfully as she walked behind the counter.

Ricky embraced her, gave her a kiss, and held her tight for a moment, then let her go.

She smiled, and enjoying his strong arms and his embrace, not ashamed to hold her in front of their friends.

She put her purse and her jacket under the counter, grabbed a cup and filled it with hot coffee, reached under the counter, grabbed the menu's, some paper and motioned to Ricky all in one motion. He followed her to a table near new the back of the restaurant and both sat down. " Well," asked Rita, what did you and Queen Emily figure out for today's luncheon menu? When they had finished hand printing the menus, they were

8

sitting there engaged in idle talk when Ricky realized he had forgotten to tell her some news he had heard this morning. "Go ahead and tell me before you 'blow a gasket'", she smiled

"Okay, here it is, I understand that our good friend, Bill Freeway has accepted the position as Police Chief of our thriving metropolis."

"That's great," she exclaimed, "I don't believe they could have selected anyone better."

At 10:10 AM the swearing in of the new Police Chief of Rogersville, Alabama was complete.

The Mayor penned the badge on his lapel and shook his hand and said, "Congratulations, Bill, welcome aboard." Bill nodded, shook the hands of the three councilmen and one councilwoman.

Bill, who tired of pomp and circumstance very easily, moved to the hall door, turned and told everyone he better get to his office and introduce himself to his staff.

Andy Hale was rewarded by his loving wife this morning by letting him sleep in because they had stayed up late with the youth at church. GOD had rewarded them with a son who grew up straight and tall. He had planned to go on a two-year mission for his church but he wanted to serve his country first, so regardless of his parent's objections, he joined the Army.

He was shipped to Iraq seven months later. They received many letters and pictures from him describing what was going on then, one day there was a knock on their front door. Ann went to answer it and Andy heard her scream. He bolted to where she lay crying uncontrollably.

Two men in army uniforms were outside the screen door. One was a captain, the other was a Major, but Andy could see he was a Chaplain.

And his heart sank, because he knew what it meant. Their one and only son was dead, killed by roadside bomb, he learned. That was two years ago, but the memory was still fresh in his mind.

Paul Mc Andrew tried sleeping late but, after many years of rising early in his position as a 'gentleman's gentleman', he now had a hard time sleeping past 5 AM. So he was awake when the special delivery letter came. He was slightly

11

surprised, but he signed for it opened it and read it with a big smile on his face. "Great", he said out loud, "the time has finally come." He almost jumped with joy, but, his training and many years of being what was one expected him to be, he rushed into his bedroom and began packing,

---

Marjorie, wife of Pete Edwards, really didn't need to work, because Pete's electrical business was going great now. However, being an old friend of Rita's for many years, she was helping her, because good help was hard to find.

On this particular day, the local postman had stopped by the restaurant for a cup of coffee and mentioned to Marjorie that he had a registered letter for her and for Pete.

Marjorie asked," Do I need to sign?" "Yes ma'am, you certainly do," as he pulled out the letter and presented it to her.

She sighed and then opened the letter, slowly reading it. The look on her face changed from quizzical to a great big smile. She let out a yell, grabbed her
purse, started out the front door, hurrying past Ricky and Rita and said " back in a little while" Then she was out the door and gone.

When she was outside, she grabbed her cell phone, dialed Pete, and when he answered , she said in a very demanding tone, " Pete, I'll be home in five minutes, be there, it's very important." Then she hung up and jumped in her car.

13

Pete stood in a stunned state for a few seconds, trying to comprehend what Marjorie could be so excited about. He remembered the last time she done this. She had just left the Doctors office when she had found out she was pregnant that the age of 36 years and she was quite upset.

Pete almost changed his mind about going home, but he knew he should, so he told his foreman that he had a problem at home and needed to get it there pronto!

He pushed the truck a little faster than he usually would in the city streets, but he was anxious to see what the problem was with Marjorie.

He pulled into the circular drive, jumped out of his pickup, dashed up the walkway, and just as he reached to unlock the door, it swung open.

There stood Marjorie, with a big smile on her face, then she grabbed Pete, and gave him a big hug, and holding him, she started dancing up and down all around the room. Pete, with both of his arms pinned to his chest, could do nothing but follow along.

Finally, he persuaded her to stop and tell him what all the excitement was about. She caught her breath and said excitedly, "We have won an all 'expenses paid' vacation for two weeks to the glorious Monte Rialto Lodge in beautiful North Alabama.

"Are you sure you want to go," asked Pete ,"remember the last time we planned a vacation."

"I know, I know," said Marjorie," but that was unexpected. Rita got terribly sick and was hospitalized and Ricky needed me to run the restaurant for him."

"Well, they are our best friends and we sure can't do enough for them" Pete asked, "when do we have to be at this resort?

"We all meet at the train depot, Saturday night, June 1, at 6 PM", replied Marjorie.

"What do you mean we all meet," asked Pete.

 "Apparently, they're more winners in town than just us," said Marjorie.,

---

"John there's a knock at the door," Ruth called out from the kitchen.

"Yeah, I heard it," John answered as he slipped on his shoes, and started for the front door. The knock came again and John said," Hold on, I'm coming!"

John opened the door and there stood the postman.

"Morning, Joe," said John.

"Morning, John," said the postman, "how are you and Ruth doing this fine morning?"

"Tolerable, just tolerable," answered John.

"Well, that's good," chuckled Joe," I've got a special delivery you need to sign for"

"Hmm, wonder who's sending us something so special we need to sign for."

"Well, just sign right here", said Joe, as he pointed to the sign line on the card.

John signed, and Joe gave him the letter and said, "Makes you feel kind of special, don't it, John? " and as he turned to walk off the porch, he said over his shoulder, " "have a good day, John."

John responded, "   Thanks and the same to you, my friend."

"Who was it,"   called Ruth, from the kitchen.

"It was the postman," answered John.

"My goodness, what did he want?"

"We've got a special delivery, along with a sales paper, and the water bill."

"Who is it from," she asked.

"Well, I don't know, I was busy reading this sales paper from Bamberger's Discount store," he replied

"Give it to me then," she snatched it out of his hand, looked at the envelope for a moment, and tore off one end, and removed the contents. As she read the letter, her face brightened, and then she let out a whoop!

"John, John guess what," she yelled, "o' happy days!", as she started dancing around the living room. "Hold on, hold on," John grabbed her, "tell me the good news, are we now millionaires?"

"No, nothing like that, but we have one to four weeks at one of the best lodges in the country with all expenses paid!"

"We have got to be at the train depot on Saturday night, June 1, at 6 PM." "Well," John replied," you better mark it on the calendar. You know how forgetful you are."

William "Bill" freeway signed, thanked the postman, and opened the envelope. He read the contents, made a mental note of the time, place and date of the important meeting, refolded the letter, put it into his pocket, and continued to his destination.

Matthew Grayson had just finished breakfast at his motel apartment, when there was a light knock at the door and he walked to it and asked, "Yes, who is it?"

A female voice from the other side replied, "Mr. Grayson, I am your post-lady and I have a special delivery letter that you must sign for."

He opened the door and signed for the long awaited letter. He was beginning to wonder if he was going to have to make a few telephone calls, but just in time, it came.

He didn't even open the letter as he knew what was in it. He opened his briefcase, and inserted the letter in it. Then he relaxed on the bed, and now he was satisfied, things were finally on the way as he had planned.

Most of the people arrived before 6:00 P.M. and were sitting quietly, when a well- dressed gentleman entered, shut the door gently, and surveyed the room, and then walked to the front, laid his briefcase on the table, and opened it with a loud click of the locks.

The man was in his early 30's, and his eyes seem to rest on Mr. Matthew Grayson a few moments longer than the other invitees, but, then, quickly looked away

He clasped his hands, and spoke. "Ladies and Gentlemen, let me introduce myself. My name is Lee Blaze and I am here to tell you all some wonderful news."

Several people raised their hands as if they had questions, whereby Blaze raised both hands and said, "Please, please, there will be time for questions later."

"Please let me call out the names and see if everyone is present." He reached into his briefcase and pulled out a piece of paper and began calling out the names, and satisfied they were all there, he returned the paper back to his briefcase,

"Now, great, all are here, and say, I forgot, there is hot coffee, ice water, soft drinks, and lemonade, if you prefer, on the side-board, if you're thirsty.

Again, he looked around the room, smiled, and started his presentation. You have been selected to spend two fabulous weeks in one of the most luxurious hotels in the world. It will be an 'all expenses' paid holiday for all of you. It will be a vacation like no one has ever had before!"

A ripple of excitement went through the room, just as expected.

"That sounds great, doesn't it," he asked.

"You can swim, fish, water ski, boat ride, get a tan, or just loaf all day if you want, it's entirely up to you, and it's all paid for. Oh, and I left out something, there's also a nine-hole golf course."

Bill Freeway stood up and said, "I think it's time for some questions."

"Why yes, Mr. Freeway, go right ahead," answered Blaze.

"Mr. Blaze," started Bill, "you're painting a mighty pretty picture and all but there are some things on my mind. Number 1, who is paying for all this and number 2, why us?"

There was a murmur in the crowd, and several shook their heads in agreement.

Blaze thanked Freeway and said, "I don't blame you for being suspicious of something such as this, I would be too probably. But, in this case, I want you to understand that the person that is doing this is doing it because he wants to do it, and right now, that's about all I can tell you."

Pete Edwards asked, "This isn't one of those deals where they try to sell you part of a condo, or land or something, is it?"

"Oh, no, nothing like that, I assure you. No fast talking sales people at all."

"Well, that's a relief," said Pete.

There was laughter all around the room, including Blaze.

"Is there anyone here tonight that doesn't feel they would enjoy a vacation such as this," Blaze asked.

There was a lot of talk in the room; husbands talking to wives, wives talking to wives, men to men, and some were just sitting there quietly listening to the others.

"Alright, please, settle down", Blaze asked, "let's finish." He reached into his briefcase again, and pulled out a form, about the size of an ordinary letter.

When they had all settled down, he said, "Unfortunately, with the good, there is the not so bad. I have to read these set of rules to you, then have you sign that you understand, and will abide by them."

"Okay, here we go. Rule number 1, is that you will not, and I stress the word, not, discuss this free vacation with anyone, not even your family!"

"Wait a minute, there Lee," said Andy, "we can't tell anyone about our good fortune?"

"No sir, Mr. Hale," replied Blaze, "however, you may discuss it all you like amongst yourselves, but let me caution you and stress this as hard as I can, 'with no one else',"

"What happens if we do," asked Marjorie Edwards.

Blaze turned the page and read the answer, 'If at any time, any invitee discusses or mentions this holiday jaunt to anyone outside of the chosen group, then the complete package will cancelled and no one shall be able to enjoy said holiday without full payment."

Blaze looked the room over, observing the group, who sat quietly, as if waiting for someone else to speak.

"Does everyone understand this rule? It's very important for all of you. You cannot tell or talk to anyone outside of the people in this room," continued Blaze.

Paul McAndrew and Matthew Grayson sat quietly, observing the others. Both had been in this area for about six months, and had made friends with them all, hopefully making lasting friendships.

Matthew Grayson nor Paul McAndrew, never, ever, let on just how wealthy Grayson really was.

All the townspeople knew was that he was a retiree, settling in their hometown. They all treated him and Paul real well, however they had no idea that Paul was his valet for many, many years.

He nudged Paul, "Ask Mr. Blaze, what is rule number 2."

Paul stood up and because of his soft voice he had to call Blaze twice before he was recognized.

"Yes, Mr. McAndrew," said Blaze.

"Please read rule number 2," he asked politely.

"Ah, rule number 2 states that no animals shall accompany the invitees."

"But, Mr. Blaze," Marjorie Edwards almost shouted, "we have a poodle that's never spent more than a day away from us and I'm afraid of what it will do to her."

"I'm sorry, Mrs. Edwards," said Blaze, sorrowfully, "I have a pet dog that I truly love also, so I know exactly what you are talking about, but again, that's the rules, and I didn't set them. I'm only here to make sure you know and understand them before we break up tonight."

Marjorie had a very sad look on her face almost as if she was about to cry, when Pete stood up, put his arm around her and gently forced her back into her chair.

Blaze wondered how could one man give so much joy, yet, on one hand cause such sadness on the other.

"Okay, rule number 3 and this is the last and maybe the most important one. Rule number 3 states, 'If any one person or a couple, decide that they will not, cannot, or do not want to participate, then it automatically cancels all the invitations for all remaining invitees."

Ricky Roberts was the first to jump up, "You mean that if someone has a serious illness, or becomes bed ridden, that ends it for all of us?"

"Yes, sir, I'm afraid so. But, please let's pray that never happens. If someone cannot make the trip, then, maybe you can all meet and try to solve the problem. Now, I know you can't do anything about something as serious as a heart attack, but there are other problems that will surely pop up that can be solved between all of you."

"Say, that's a good idea," Matthew Grayson finally spoke, "if we see there might be a problem, then we can call a special meeting, and we can discuss and maybe iron out a solution amongst ourselves. Frankly, I do not want to lose this holiday, because I've never been able to afford one such as this." He thought he saw the head of Blaze jerk around towards him, but he didn't let on as if he noticed.

"Sounds good to me," said Freeway, and several others chimed in also.

"Alright then," said Blaze, "if I can get everyone to come up here and sign this, as accepting the rules, then that will be all for tonight."

Alma Hale asked as she signed, "When do we meet again?"

Blaze clapped his hands, drawing attention to him-self once more, "Yes, thank you Mrs. Hale, I

32

almost forgot. We meet again, on August 1, at 6:00 P.M. Please remember this, you all must be here or it's all called off, cancelled!"

After everyone had signed the form, the people were just standing around chatting with each other, when Blaze excused himself, stepped out the door, and was gone.

CHAPTER 2

The telephone rang once, twice, three times before he finally decided to answer, and when he did, he simply said, "Hello."

He paused, listening to the familiar voice on the other end, then he said, "Why, yes, thank you for asking. I've just downed the last of my pills."

He paused again, listening, then, "I thank so too. The meeting went about as I expected. I think Mr. Blaze did a terrific job. I was very impressed by his presentation."

Again he waited, "Well, of course, the whole idea is to get them to come, and as a group or none at all, and…"

The voice on the other end interrupted, and this almost ticked him off, but he let his usually bad temper fade away this time.

The voice, realizing he had interrupted, stopped talking immediately, and waited for the fiery cursing that was forthcoming. So he braced himself, because he had done the unpardonable sin, he had interrupted the man, and you, never, ever did that either in public or private. If you did there were dire consequences to pay.

The voice waited, but nothing. Had he hung up? No, he heard him breathing, or at least he thought he did, dare he speak?

He finally decided to be brave and break the silence, "Sir," he said, apologetically.

After a moment, the man answered, "Yes, I'm here. As I was saying, I believe that the all or none rule got through to them, don't you think?

The voice, in a relieved tone answered, "Yes sir, oh, yes sir, I agree with you 100% about that. It really hit home to the, all or nothing."

"Without all of them," the man continued, "my plan will never work to my satisfaction. Don't you agree?"

The voice paused for a moment, and then answered, "But sir, don't you believe that some is better than none?"

"No, not in this case," he said slowly, "it must be the ones that I have selected. They are the prime targets, and are the major parts of the plan.

However, the others can, and will be allowed to back out if necessary."

"And if they don't?"

"Then I have made the necessary plans for them also when the reach the hotel, I have thought this through and through, and I cannot see any errors in it whatsoever, can you?"

"No sir, I cannot either, only one of the group bothers me, and that's speaking from past experience," said the voice.

"Who do you think it is," he asked.

"I believe the one to give the most trouble will be William Freeway, the current Chief of Police of Rogersville," he said.

"And why him," he asked.

"Because, he is retired from the Alabama Bureau of Investigation, being in the service for about 12 years. You know, sir, they take only the finest of the State Troopers and turn them into one of the finest crime fighting forces in the world."

"Yes, I know, but if we play our cards right, and with your experience and training, we should be able to out-fox him, don't you think?"

"I think so sir," he answered slowly, "in fact, I must."

"Yes, you must, because this means as much to you as it does to me. Do you understand?"

"Yes sir, I understand, I just hope that I can operate this business just as half as good as you have, sir," the voice said.

In a stern voice, the man answered, "I have no doubt, my boy, if I had, you would not be where you are today. I didn't work all my life just to leave all this to some groveling baby, who would eventually run it into the ground. I wanted someone with enough stamina and guts to keep it going. There are a lot of people out there who is depending on me for a living, and I am not going let them down. Now, is that clear?"

"Sir, I've known how you felt for some time now, and I will not let you down, just have faith in me, that is all I ask," the voice replied.

"I have faith in you, so don't let me down, not now or ever" replied the man, and he hung up.

"Honey, hurry, it's getting on towards time to go," Ruth yelled upstairs to her husband.

He appeared at the top of the staircase, and in about two leaping bounds, was standing beside her with a big smile on his face.

She looked at him, adjusted his tie, and said, "Careful cowboy, one of these days you're going to make a misstep and I'm going to have to scoop you up with a shovel!

He chuckled, "Let's hope that day never comes." He leaned forward, kissed her on the cheek, pinched her on the buttocks and quickly jumped towards the front door.

She yelled, swung at him, missing entirely and then pointed her finger at him, "If you don't stop that, one of these days, I'm going to break those fingers off!"

He laughed, knowing she was kidding and also knowing she was enjoying it, hurried out the door, and went and got the ten year old Chevy Malibu.

On the way, Ruth asked, "You know John we really haven't talked about this you know. What do you really think?"

"Gosh, Ruth, I'd really like to go, but do you think you could stand two weeks?"

"Yes, yes, I believe I could," she answered, "in fact, I'm really looking forward to it."

"Rita, you haven't said anything to our help about a paid vacation yet, have you," asked Ricky as they drove to the Train depot.

41

"Of course not," she answered.

"Well, make sure you don't until I can see if the bank will make us that loan to pay them, plus have some to carry with us."

She had a puzzled look on her face, "But, what if the banks won't give us that loan," she asked.

"Why shouldn't they. We have good credit with them and we've always paid on time, and we have several loans paid off on time," he said. "Honey, I'm almost positive they will give it to us, but you know how banks are. First, you have got to prove you don't need it, or want it, and maybe the Loan Officer had a bad argument with his wife before coming to work this morning, and he's not in a very good mood

Rita laughed and sat back and said, "We are going to vote yes, right?"

"You can bet your last dollar," Ricky answered as he pulled their vehicle into the parking lot of the Train Depot.

"Here comes the Edwards," said Andy Hale, "and I see the Suttons also. Maybe everyone will show up after all.

"I surely hope so," Alma said, "I called everyone and they agreed to be here tonight."

"Well, if they said they'd be here, then they'll be here. I have all the confidence in the world. But I wish they'd come on, and let's get it over with, because the Braves come on at 7:00."

"Aw, you and your ball-games," she scoffed, "you act like they may lose if you are not there watching them."

"That is a great possibility, you know," he retorted.

Several in the room, laughed when he said that, but the truth of the matter was, most wanted to get home to watch it too. The Braves were a favorite of most in Rogersville during baseball season.

The radio crackled, "PD to unit 1."

No answer. Again, "PD to unit 1."

Chief William "Bill" Freeway answered, "This is unit 1, go ahead Rosie."

"Chief, you said to call you at 5:30."

He keyed the mike and said, "Yes, I did, and thank you Rosie. I almost forgot. Say if you need me, buzz my pager."

"10-4, Chief", answered Rosie.

He'd have to finish this investigation tomorrow. Someone or somebodies broke into this warehouse and stole a very valuable Maserati sports car, according to the owner.

He surveyed the old warehouse from his patrol car, then, headed to the meeting at the Train Depot.

As they were seated, Alma Hale stood up and said, "Good evening everyone, I was hoping that Chief Freeway would be here to conduct this meeting, but apparently he is on some important police business."

Pete Edwards put his hands over his mouth and sniggered, "Yeah, probably getting Mrs. Maddie's cat out of that big oak tree."

Several laughed as they knew the many times the police and volunteer fire department had been called to retrieve her cat or cats from the big oak in her front yard.

Just then the door opened, and a big "John Wayne" type of body entered, and made his way to the front of the room, as Alma shut the door behind him.

He took off his baseball cap, looked at everyone, and said, "Sorry, I'm late, I had some police business to attend to."

Pete put his hand over his mouth again as before and said, "Didn't involve a dangerous cat and a big oak did it?"

With that, most burst out laughing, including the Chief.

When they had settled down, the Chief said, "I wish it had been that simple, but no, no cat call today, thank goodness."

"Friends, I'd like to be quite frank with you. The Atlanta Braves come on at 7:00 P.M. and I sure don't want to miss any of it," he said

"Amen," said Andy Hale and echoed by John Sutton and Pete Edwards. Even Matthew Grayson was seen to nod his head.

"To make it short and sweet, is there any one here that does not, or maybe foresee any problems or complications with all of us accepting this generous offer," asked Freeway

Freeway looked around the room, and his eyes rested on the room, and they rested on Paul Mc Andrew.

"Mr. McAndrew, you've been mighty quite, how about a word or two from you," asked Bill.

Paul set there for a moment, aware that all of their eyes were upon him. He was in the spotlight, and that was something he did not relish at all or like whatsoever.

Grayson spoke up, "Yes, Paul, I think we'd like to know what you think and feel about all of this."

Paul gave Grayson the old stare, 'I'll get you for this" and started to speak, but only stammered.

Freeway spoke up, "Paul, please stand up, where we can hear."

Paul stood, very aware that all were watching him, coughed, and finally said without stammering, "I think we all should accept this generous offer. I think we all should vote yes, and we should all go and truly enjoy ourselves." Then he sat down.

Freeway clapped his hands lightly and said, "Thanks, Paul, I certainly agree with you, and if there is no further discussion, we all agree to go!"

"Who is the appointed person to contact Mr. Blaze," asked Freeway.

The people began to look around at each other, asking the same question.

Finally, Grayson stood up, and said to Freeway, and the others, "Did any of you give your address or telephone number to Mr. Blaze?"

Everyone either said no, or shook their heads in the negative

"Neither did I, so what I suggest is this, just sit back and wait, and maybe he will contact one of us."

"But, we have only have thirty-one days to let him know," said Ruth Sutton.

"Yes, that's true," echoed several others.

Most shook their heads in agreement with Ruth, but what was there to do?

Freeway held up his hands to quiet the crowd, and when that was accomplished, he said, "I'll tell you what I will do. If we don't hear from Mr.

Blaze pretty quick, say in a week or so, then I will get on the phone to the A.B.I. and see if they can locate him for us, how about that?"

Everyone seemed to agree, and Matthew Grayson stood up and said, "I have a strong feeling that Mr. Blaze will indeed contact Mr. Freeway within the next week or so. I just have that feeling."

Everyone turned to look at Grayson and the way he said it convinced them all that Mr. Blaze would indeed contact Bill Freeway with a week or so.

The meeting broke up, and everyone left chatting with one another, the women talking of what they were going to wear, the men just listening and running dollar figures through their minds at the new out fits they were going to have to pay for.

CHAPTER 3

""Ruth," John yelled, "we've got another special delivery letter. Do you want me to sign or do you want to?"

"My goodness, John," Ruth yelled, "ask Joe if you can sign without me, and if so, just sign the darn thing!"

"Joe, did you hear that?"

"Couldn't help but too," answered Joe, "'imagine half the folks in the county heard it too."

John sniggered, but not too loud, he didn't want Ruth to hear, "Please let me sign for that thing."

"You know John, the Postmaster said a bunch of these came in today," said Joe.

"Really, maybe we all won a free trip to the moon for a hundred payments of only $9.99 per month."

"Ha," laughed Joe, "that's probably true, alright, said Joe as he tore off the slip and gave John his letter. Then he turned and was on his way.

John hurried into the house, went over to his favorite chair, sat down and waited on Ruth, and in a few moments, here she was standing next to him, drying her hands on her apron, and asked, "Is that what we have been expecting?

"Could be," he answered, "Joe said there was a lot of them being delivered around town today."

"Really, then that's really great news, maybe we all can now make our plans to go."

John carefully opened up the large envelope and looked in.

"Hurry up," she said, and shook his arm, "hurry up."

Frustrated, he handed the envelope to her, "Here, you do it."

She took it from him, removed all the contents, and carefully spread them on the table beside his chair. There was an introductory letter, a credit card, a brochure about the lodge, and a plastic key with a number on it.

That's all? She turned the envelope upside down, expecting something else to fall out but, nothing did.

"Hmmm," she said, and then put on her glasses, picked up the letter, and sat down in her favorite chair and began to read.

The letter told what each item was for. The key was the number of their room, the credit card was for a gasoline fill-up at the National Convenience Store on the edge of town, good for one time only, and a brochure that described the wonders of the Monte Rialto Hotel, and a map showing the route from Rogersville to the Hotel. In the last paragraph, it stated that check-in would begin at

11:00 A.M. and would close at 8:00 P.M. Please check in during those hours, thank you!

"Wow," exclaimed John, absolutely impressed with the brochure, "I just can't wait."

Ruth gathered up all the contents, put them back in the envelope, and asked John, "Now, where shall we put this?"

"No better place than our family bible, "answered John.

"Okay, watch me," as she walked over to the large bookcase against the wall, reached up and extracted a large black copy of the King James Version of the Holy Bible, opened it, and placed the envelope inside.

There were a lot of happy people around town tonight because they had opened their envelopes, that is, all but the Police Chief, William "Bill" Freeway. Oh, he had signed for it alright, but he just hadn't had the time to stop and open it in private. Right now, it was the least of his worries.

He had just been called to an old warehouse owned by Mr. Rogers, the same man who had the Maserati stolen from his other warehouse.

This time, it was apparently a warehouse full of color televisions, stereos, microwaves, and other electronic gadgets. Mr. Rogers was adamant that he had the only keys and that someone had broken in both places, but truthfully, Bill could not find any signs of forced entry in either warehouse.

Bill was sitting at his desk, reached for his glass of cold ice water, took a large swallow, then called for Jack Wilson, his Assistant Chief.

"He's already gone home Chief," answered Rosie, the dispatcher.

He looked up at the old clock on the wall, and sure enough it was 6:30 P.M. Everybody was gone but himself, Rosie and Robert, the early night shift patrolman.

"Okay, thank you," he yelled back.

He decided to head home, so he locked his desk, picked up the letter, and started out the door.

He stopped at the door for a moment, turned and walked into the dispatcher office, just as Robert was heading out the door.

Rosie had a small FM radio on, not too loud, but where she could hear it okay. She had a sandwich in her hand, and was concentrating on the song emanating from the radio.

"Rosie," he said.

Rosie jumped, almost falling out of her chair, and coming up in a defensive posture, ready to take the Chief out.

She recognized him and said, her voice shaking somewhat, "Chief, you almost turned this black lady whiter than you are!"

Chief Freeway started laughing at what she said, and then, "Rosie, I swear I didn't mean to startle you. Please forgive me."

"Whoooe me," said Rosie. I thought you had gone."

"I started to go, but then I thought of a question that maybe you can help me with."

By this time, Rosie had set back down, and Freeway had told her to continue eating.

"Chief, you don't mind," she asked.

"No, as long as it doesn't interfere with your duties," he answered, "I have no objections."

"Thanks, Chief. Say, what did you want to ask me."

"Rosie, you were born and raised here in Rogersville, weren't you?"

"Yes sir, about 27 years ago," she answered.

"This town was probably named after the Rogers family, don't you think?"

"Yes, they said in the old days, most of Rogersville used to be a pretty big cotton plantation and after the Civil War, well they fell on hard times and some of the land was sold off. But, one of the sons took over and brought it back, and I think it was Mr. Rogers Daddy that did it, but he died."

"You're talking about the Rogers that owns the electronics store, aren't you," asked the Chief.

"Unfortunately, Chief, that's it. The richest family in the state at one time. And who knows about now. A run-down store, a twenty year old car, and a mansion that's already fallen in, and the wood burned as scrap."

"Thanks, Rosie," he said, starting to leave, "you have answered a lot of questions for me, and tomorrow, I'm going to do something that a lots of folks in this town may not like."

The next day being Monday, he walked into his office, nothing important, so he walked down the hall to the dispatcher's office.

Jimmy, the daytime dispatcher was on duty, and Bill asked for last night's radio log. Jimmy hadn't filed it yet, so when Bill read it, it contained the usual things, barking dogs, shadows in the night, loud noises, and he was just about to hand it back to Jimmy, when he noticed, "Light on in Rogers Electronics-11:30 P.M."

Bill asked Jimmy, "What is so important to have a patrolman check on a light in Rogers Electronics at 11:30 P.M.?

"Well, Chief, I believe, it's because it's well known that Mr. Rogers is such a miser, that he dares not to leave any lights on in his store after closing, so Robert may have thought something was wrong, I guess," Jimmy explained.

"Okay, I see. That was good police work by Robert. A lot of men would have just let that slip by, or ignored it," said the Chief.

He went into his office, called Rosie, and apologized for waking her up, but, he had a very important question.

"Rosie, what was so important about Robert checking on a light in Rogers Electronics?"

"He was patrolling along and he saw a light in the back office, and knowing Mr. Rogers, how a miser he is, and knowing he would never ever, leaves lights on, he thought there might be a chance of foul play, so he stopped, and checked, but could find nothing wrong, " said Rosie.

"How did he know there was no foul play," asked the Chief.

"He checked both doors, and they were locked and no sign anywhere of forced entry," she answered, sleepily.

"What else did you and Robert do?"

"Well, he got me to call the store to see if anyone was in there, and I did, but no answer, so we figured he just left the light on, this one time," said Rosie, with a yawn.

"Okay, Rosie thanks, go back to sleep now." He hung up and decided to go down to Rogers Electronics.

When he pulled into the parking spot in front of the store, he sat there for a few minutes, surveying the front of what looked like an empty building.

He finally decided to go in, but when he tried the front door, it was locked to his surprise. Then he seen the small sign on the front showing that the opening time was 9:00 A.M. He looked at his watch, it was only 7:45, and his stomach told him he wanted breakfast.

He was eating a plate of eggs, sausage, grits, and biscuits, sitting in a corner table, when the owner, Ricky Roberts walked over.

"Mind if I sit with you for a while," he asked.

"No, of course not," replied the Chief, "make your self at home.

Ricky sat down, and asked, "How is your breakfast."

"Fine and dandy," he answered, "these biscuits just melt in your mouth."

"Yes, that's our cook, Queen Emily, we call her, is one of the best cooks in this country and she's been with us ever since we opened up," Ricky said.

"Question? What are you going to do with your business when you leave on the vacation," asked Freeway.

"We're planning to let them off on a two weeks paid vacation. They have certainly earned it," Ricky answered.

"They ought to really enjoy that, and say, did you get what I got in the mail?"

"Yes, sir, we did, and can hardly wait," answered Ricky.

Freeway laughed lightly, laid down a tip for Rita, his waitress, and started towards the cashier to pay his ticket, but Ricky snatched it out of his hand.

"Hey, what are you doing," asked Bill.

"Just consider this as my investment towards law-enforcement in our great town," said Ricky, as he walked away.

Chief Freeway looked at his watch as he got into his patrol car and it was only 8:45, still 15 minutes to go.

He decided to ride down the alley behind the stores, barely creeping along, especially behind

Rogers Electronics. He stopped, and could see the light was on. He then pulled around front, parked and went to the front door, and tried to enter. But, the door was still locked.

He knocked loudly, then a little louder, and Bob Marter, the Druggist came hurrying out of his pharmacy, which was next door to Rogers Electronics, and saying, "My goodness, Chief, what's all the racket?"

"Mr. Marter, I think something is wrong with Mr. Rogers and I need to get in his store. As you can see, he's over 30 minutes late in opening, and there's a light on in the back of the store," the Chief said as he looked through the windows.

Bob Marter leaned against the front windows and said, "I see what you mean, he's never failed to open on time, and he has never as long as I've known him ever left a light on in his store!"

The Chief looked at Marter and asked, "Didn't I hear you bought this whole building from him not too long ago?"

"Yes, I did. Why," asked Marter.

"Well, sir, you can give me permission to break the lock and enter the premises, because I believe that there's been foul play!"

"I don't know Chief," Marter said, shaking his head slowly, "I just don't know about that. What if you're wrong?"

"If I'm wrong, I'll take the blame, and pay for all damages," said the Chief, "now how about that?"

Marter thought for a moment, then said, "Okay, we'll work it that way. I hope that there's nothing wrong though."

"Mr. Marter, I'll need you to be my witness, when I enter the store. I need you to stay with me step by step, understand?"

Marter answered, "Yes, Chief, I understand"

The Chief walked over to the door and give it one big shove and it cracked and popped, then the doors swung open. The two men slowly walked to the back of the dimly lit store and when they got to the closed door in the back, they could see through the window that a man's body lay crumpled on the floor.

Marter said, excitedly, "Chief, that looks like Rogers!"

The Chief slowly opened the door and was greeted with a smell that seemed as if it was coming from a very old outhouse. This odor, he knew, told him Rogers was dead, as the body had emptied itself of urine and feces.

Marter said, "Gosh, Chief, it stinks like crazy in there, shut that door!"

The Chief shut the door, then asked Marter, "Could you see his face well enough to recognize him as Rogers?"

"Oh yes, that was him all right, do doubt what so ever," answered Marter.

By this time there were a few people that had gathered at the front door, and Bill told Marter to go back to his Pharmacy and call the Coroner.

When Marter had left, Bill walked up to the crowd, he was deluged with questions, but he shrugged them off. He picked out the biggest, and tallest man in the crowd, and quickly deputized him as a volunteer patrolman. He told his new man to keep all people out of the store until his men get here.

H walked to his patrol car, called Jimmy, the dispatcher, and told him to get Jack Wilson, the Assistant Chief, Patrolman Baggett, and Patrolman Jacky Parker to come there with all haste, but not under the blue light or siren. We do not want to attract any more attention than we have too!"

"10-4, Chief," came the reply.

He went back into the store and put a handkerchief over his nose and entered the back room. Being extra careful not to touch anything, he walked around the room, trying to see if there was any clue as to why he might have died.

Not seeing anything out of the ordinary, such as blood spilled on the floor, or a big bruise on the back of the head, or bullet holes in the walls, he went back into the store front., and as he shut the door, he heard someone arguing with his temporary patrolman.

He walked to the door, and there was Doctor McKenzie, trying to get past the man, but he wouldn't let him through.

The Doctor seen the Chief, and said, "Chief, will you please tell this big lummock that I am the county Coroner, and I must get through to examine the body!"

Bill touched the man on the shoulder and said, "Let him through, and keep up the good work."

The man smiled and turned back to guard the store, as Bill and the Doctor made their way to the back, Bill said, "Doc, you better put on a surgical mask, if you have one, because the odor is pretty strong."

Later, the Doctor said, "It looks like a heart attack to me, but you know under state law, I'll have to do an autopsy, to be sure."

"Yeah, Doc, I know," said the Chief, "please let me know the results when you get them, okay?"

By this time, Jack and the other patrolmen had arrived and Bill told Jack to take pictures of the dead body from all angles, and anything else he thought might be useful.

He told the patrolmen to replace the locks on the door , put yellow police tape across the front and back door, and help the morgue attendants when they came to retrieve the body.

Both of the young patrolmen had a squeamish look on their face when Bill told them this, so he asked, "You guys seem like you are not in favor of that idea."

Both of them started shuffling their feet a little, and then Baggett said, "To tell you the truth Chief, I've never had any dealings with a dead body. The closest I've ever come is at a funeral and that was close enough!"

Bill laughed at their predicament, and said, "Look, men, the body is dead, and it can't hurt you at all. Just be there if they need you, and maybe, just maybe, they won't."

Both of the men seemed relieved and nodded their heads. Bill right then knew he had to set up an appointment for them with Doctor McKenzie, at one of his autopsies. All policemen and policewomen should view this procedure.

CHAPTER 4

Just as Bill was about to leave, he noticed the Doctor coming out of the store, and he called out to him, "Say, Doc, are you hungry?"

"Chief, my friend, can you not tell by the size of my middle, that I like to eat or not. This mid-section is not from drinking beer!"

The Chief laughed, and said, "Can you follow me up to the Robert's Restaurant, it's my treat?"

"Don't get in my way, I might run over you," was the reply.

Later, when they were seated and had been served, Bill asked just how well, did he know Rogers?

"I knew him pretty well, at least ever since he came back from the Korean War. He was a P.O.W you know," said the Doctor, between bites.

"No, I didn't know that," answered Bill.

"If you have time, I can tell you a sad story about the man, that a lot of people in this town thought was crazy, but he wasn't, no not by a long shot," said the Doctor.

"I've got the time if you do, that is you can spare it," replied Bill.

"Chief, you know as a Doctor, I hear and see a lot of things that I can't repeat, just like Priests, lawyers and such. Rogers might be the last of a long, long line, or he may not be. I'll tell you about it in a minute."

"But first, let's see if we can get us another piece of that delicious peach pie and a cold glass of milk."

Bill was beginning to wonder just how much food one man could hold, but after two more pieces of pie and another cup of coffee, the

Doctor, belched, apologized and started the story

about Albert Walker Rogers, Jr., late owner of

Rogers Electronics and the Rogers Plantation. The

doctor leaned back in his chair and began.

It was beginning to turn into spring, the trees

and flowers were starting to bloom, and sweet

smells filled the air.

Wilma Rogers raised her bedroom window on

the second floor of the Rogers Plantation home

and inhaled the sweet, sweet odor emanating from

the tulip tree just outside her bedroom.

"Oh, how wonderful," she thought, "how great

it is to be alive. To be married to a handsome,

successful man whom I adore with all my heart

and soul."

She heard a sound, looked down and saw her husband's late model Ford roll up the driveway, then stop at the front door. Her husband stepped out.

She yelled from her window, "Hello, sweetheart."

He looked up, and yelled back at her, "Why, hello yourself, you beautiful creature!"

She hurried downstairs and into his arms. They hugged tightly, and she led him to the kitchen.

"Annie," she said to their cook, for thirty years, "have you got our darling boy some lunch. He looks mighty hungry."

Annie laughed, "Yes'm, I got his favorite meal fixed today. I's got baked ham and cheese sandwiches, hot homemade vegetable soup, and a big jug of lemonade." Annie stood there, smiling.

Albert stood, dead still, "Now, wait a minute. Something's going on here. You two are ganging up on me, I can feel it."

Neither Wilma nor Annie spoke a word, but Albert wasn't convinced. He knew that look on Annie's face. He'd seen it before over his past twenty-five years, that grin from ear to ear, showing pearly white teeth.

"Alright you two, I'll not consume a bite until you two grinning hyenas tell me what's going on!"

With that, Wilma said, "Okay then Annie, just put it all up. The master decides not to partake of this wonderful luncheon that you have prepared for him."

"Yes'm," said Annie, and made a move to remove the food and drink from the table,

Albert drew back his hand as if to strike Annie on the hand if she touched the food and said, "Do it, Annie, and you'll draw back a nub!"

Annie laughed and withdrew her big hands and said, "Mr. Albert, you wouldn't do that, now would you, but you'd better sit down and eat. There is some field hands that would like to get hold on this."

Wilma sat down at the table and Annie brought her a bowl of soup and a large glass of lemonade.

She and Albert held hands, said the blessing, and looking directly into his eyes, she said softly, "You know, that Dr. Johnson stopped by this morning on his regular run."

"Yes," said, Albert, "did you get the examination that we talked about?"

"Yes, oh yes, he did that," she said slowly>

After a few moments of silence, it finally dawned on him, that she had something to tell him, so he stopped chewing, stopped breathing, and looked her straight in the eyes, and stammering said, "Wha—wha—what did, did, he say?

Wilma smiled, "He said that there's a ninety percent chance that you're soon to be a poppa!"

"Woweeee," he yelled, and grabbed her out of her chair, and grabbed Annie and they started dancing around and around!

When he got back to his office, he marked the date on his calendar, May 6, 1925.

83

Of course, Wilma had told him, she had to pass the 'rabbit test' to make sure that she was really pregnant. She passed it, and soon she had a beautiful boy, but unfortunately, he came down with pneumonia, and died after three weeks.

Albert and Wilma were, of course, heart-broken, and it seemed that she would never quite recover from the loss. For a long time, she just walked around in a daze, not really caring for herself.

One morning, she awoke, lying in bed, and thinking about her small child that she had lost. Maybe GOD wanted him for an angel, and she being a CHRISTian, she began to believe this. She scrambled out of bed, dressed, hurried out to the rose garden, where the many different colored

84

roses were in bloom, and sat down on the concrete seat. She smelled the rose, heard the birds singing, and then she closed her etes, then she prayed like she had never prayed before.

Soon, the Doctor happily reported to Albert and Wilma, that she was pregnant again, and when it was born, extreme medical care would be provided for the baby,

Even, Albert, if he had a sniffle, she would not let him close. No one was allowed close, if she thought even a little, that they may be sick.

One day after her third birthday, her mom decided that they should lay down in the mother's bed and take an afternoon nap.

They went upstairs to mommy and daddy's bedroom to sleep, but first, Wilma made sure that the guard-gate across the stairs was securely in place. It was designed to keep the little girl off the stairs.

Wilma and her sweet little child, whom she had named Judith, after her mother, laid down and soon Judith was sound asleep.

Wilma soon drifted off, and she thought she was dreaming, because she heard a scream, and then, Annie was calling her.

She awoke, and realized it was no dream. She reached for Judith, and she was not there. Where was she?

Again she heard the scream, "Miz Wilma, oh, please come here!"

The urgency in Annie's voice made her jump off the bed and rush out of the bedroom, and head to the stairs, and couldn't believe what she saw.

There was Annie, crying her heart out, and in her arms, was the limp body of her darling daughter, Judith.

Later, it was determined that the child had tried to climb over the gate, and possibly caught her foot, and fell down the stairs, breaking her neck.

Wilma walked around for months, as if in a trance, losing weight that she couldn't afford to lose.

Annie tried to get her to eat by cooking her favorite meals, but she would only nibble at them, eating very little.

Albert, of course was worried, and was just about at his wits end on what to do. He had tried to get her interested in gardening, or reading, or something to get her mind off the tragedy, but no luck.

One day, he was reading the paper in his office and he seen an advertisement for a cruise, leaving out of Mobile, and it would be at sea for seven days. It had dances, plenty of food, a swimming pool on board and many other things to keep its patrons occupied.

He called his secretary into his office and told her to see when and if the train went to Mobile, in conjunction with the Gulf of Mexico cruise, and if so, to purchase tickets for two, on both.

Now, he faced the problem of talking her into

going on this trip, and maybe, he had just the right

way to do it. She, before she lost the children,

loved to shop for new clothes, and he decided to

take her to Montgomery, to one of the large

department stores to purchase a complete new

wardrobe just for this trip.

When he had her sit down, and he looked into

her deep, far-away eyes, he started to explain what

he wanted to do. But, she refused, as he expected

her to do, so he told her in no uncertain terms, that

she was going to shop, and she was going on the

cruise, even if he had to tie her up and drag her

with him.

Her eyes grew wide, and she got up, without a

word, and began dressing, to go to Montgomery.

This encouraged Albert, so he changed into some casual clothes, for the trip also.

They enjoyed the cruise very much, and in about nine months, Albert Walker Rogers was born. The date was July 3, 1930.

This baby was almost, as Annie would say, "the spitting image of Mr. Albert. He can't deny this young'un," and then she would laugh.

Albert Walker Rogers was indeed the very image of his father, and his mother hardly ever let the babe out of her sight. No one, absolutely no one, touched the child, except Wilma, not even Albert or Annie.

The child grew, and his mother decided to home teach him and he was a fast learner. He was working algebra problems by the time he was only eight years old and he was speaking Spanish fluently.

He had no contact with other children, so he knew no childhood games. Wilma would pitch ball with him occasionally, but she would make sure he was not over extended or getting too hot.

When he was sixteen, his father taught him how to drive over the objections of Wilma. To Wilma's surprise, this was one time Albert put his foot down, and demanded that he have the right to teach his son.

Wilma gave in, but only if they would stay on the plantation. She sat on the front porch, and watched the whole time, her fingers clenched, and her breath held for short periods of time.

He begged his parents to let him go into town by himself, and see if he could possibly meet some other boys or girls of his age. He wanted to go to the movies that he had read about, to car races, and yes to maybe a honky-tonk or two.

When he said this, Wilma almost exploded, "No, not in my lifetime, will I ever give you the okay to go into those dens of evil. There's nothing in there to see, only evil and evil women, just waiting to take your money and your soul!"

Albert Jr., looked at his Dad with a question, and Albert Sr. replied, "She's right son. You usually have to fight your way in, and fight your way out."

"Well, what about the movies," he asked, "is there any harm in going to see a show?"

"No, not really, but there are certain movies I wish you would not see. So I tell you what. I'll see what's on the local movie house, and I'll see if we can go as a family, how about that?"

That seemed to satisfy him, and he said, "Now comes the toughest part, in convincing Mom!"

The boy grew into a strong young man, because, again over Wilma's objections, he began to work around the plantation. His muscles soon began to ripple, and his skin turned to a golden brown and his blond hair was bleached even more of a blond.

Wilma, even though she didn't want to show it, was proud of Albert, Jr.

Unknown to Wilma and Albert, he had kept scrapbooks about World War II, and he would often sit down for hours and read the articles over, and over.

He admired soldiers, especially in their dress uniforms, and he imagined himself, standing erect, in full dress, with a rifle slung over his soldier.

So, on July 3, 1948, on his 18th birthday, he sneaked into town, and enlisted in the United States Army. He was now a soldier and he was proud.

That night, at supper, he gently broke the news to Albert, Sr. and Wilma. Wilma could only sit and stare at him. She was in complete shock, it seemed.

Albert Sr. was taken aback at first, then he said, "Son, are you sure this is what you want?"

Jr. said, "Yes sir, I have thought about it for some time, and this is definitely what I want to do at this time."

Just at that time, Wilma came to herself and almost screaming," I will not have it," and turning to Albert Sr., "You have got to go down there right now and demand that they release my son from this."

Albert Sr., said "My dear, I'm afraid it's too late. He's already signed all his enlistment papers, taken his physical, and now all he is doing is awaiting orders on where to report and when."

"But, they can't take my baby," she wailed, "they can't do this to me, they just can't. I won't allow it." She started crying.

Albert Jr. and Sr. never liked for Wilma to cry, so they both jumped up, went to her chair, and wrapped their arms around her and held her tight.

Nevertheless, what was done, was done, and there was nothing they could do to stop there only son from going into the U.S. Army. Secretly, Albert was very proud of his son, and when he sent home his first pictures, of him in his uniform, Albert Sr., was about to burst with pride. Wilma, was proud too, but was afraid to show it, although, he thought he saw her smile just a little while she was gazing at the picture.

While he was at Fort Benning, Georgia, they would go and see him as many times as he would allow them to come, and when they did, he would brag about how he learned to shoot rifles, pistols, the correct way to throw grenades, and the correct use of the bayonet.

To Albert Sr., this was exciting news, as he saw his son was truly enjoying what he was going through, but to Wilma, it was just more ways for her son to get hurt, and she didn't like it.

There came a time when he called and told them he was being transferred to a base in California, and he would like to see them before he left.

Wilma called Albert and told him the news, "Dear, Jr. just called and said that his unit is being transferred to a fort in California. He wants us to come over this weekend, because after then, the base will be closed to visitors. Now, why would they do that?"

Albert was silent for a moment, then answered, "Just get us ready, and tomorrow is Friday, and we'll leave early in the morning." He hung up, and turned up the radio, and finished listening to the news bulletin. North Korea, had crossed the border separating North and South Korea, and the United States, had declared they would assist the government to repel the invaders.

Yes, he knew why the base was locked down, and he knew why his son's unit was being transferred to California. He hung his head and prayed, something he had not done in a long, long time.

Jr. would call from California whenever he had the chance, and it seemed that the calls were becoming fewer and fewer. Once, he even mentioned, "I've got someone I want you to meet. I know you'll love her like I do." Then he hung with no further explanation.

This nearly drove Wilma crazy, and she nearly drove Albert crazy too, because she would continually bring up the statement Jr. had made to her. She was worried that her baby boy, was falling for another woman, and if who was she.

One morning, around 5:00 A.M, she awoke, and turned over to Albert, and shook him awake. "What do you want this early in the morning," he asked sleepily.

"I've, got an idea," she said happily, "let's go to California and see our boy."

"What", he almost yelled, "are you crazy? Or are you still asleep?"

"No, I am not," she answered defiantly, "I want to go to California. I want to see my baby. I've been listening to the news and I've been reading the papers. I know about Korea, even though you've tried hard to keep it away from me."

He sat up in bed, rubbed the sleep out of his eyes, then said, "Yes, honey, it does look bad right now, but with Gen. McArthur in charge, things will turn around, just you wait and see."

"But, I am still worried that Jr. will be part of that 'turn around' as you call it."

"Yes, that's possible, but just because he's in the Army, doesn't mean he will go to Korea", said Albert soothingly," why during World War II, many soldiers and sailors never left American soil."

"No matter, I still want to go," she insisted.

"All right, I'll see what I can do." he said, "but now how about breakfast?"

They had tried to contact Jr. before they left, but was unable to, and they also tried at each layover of the train, but was told the troops could not come to the telephone.

When they arrived in California, they went to their hotel, and immediately, called Jr., and were told he was on leave. They tried to find out where he had went, but no one knew, but he was due back in three days at 1800 hours.

They patiently waited, and at 6:00 P.M. (1800), they called, and he was able to talk for only three minutes as most of all the troops wanted to make or receive calls also.

They quickly told him they were in town, and wanted to know if they could see him.

He said to give him the telephone number of their room, and if he could, he would.

They waited for ten days and no call came. Albert was just about to tell Wilma, they would have to pack and head home, that this room was getting too expensive.

Just as he was ready to tell her, the telephone rang, and Wilma jumped and answered it. It was Jr., and he said that he couldn't leave the base, but he had explained the situation to his First Sgt., and he is allowing me to see you through the fence at Gate Number 7, for about 15 minutes, tomorrow, at 1530 (2:30 P.M.) hours.

They were there at around 1:00 P.M., standing around, with what seemed to be other parents, wives, and girlfriends. They looked through the guarded gate and could see a lot of commotion going on inside, such as the loading of tanks on trailers, boxes being loaded on trucks, and different things of that nature.

Albert didn't want Wilma to see much of that, because she would soon put two and two together, and realize that they were preparing for war, and it seemed that his son and her baby, was about to be involved in it.

Soon, Jr., and several other young soldiers crowded along the fence and there was much talking, and a lot of crying.

Wilma, asked him what did he mean about someone that he wanted them to meet?

He just held up his left hand, and showed her the ring on his finger indicating he was now married. Wilma turned pale, and asked, "Who is it, and where is she?"

Just then, a large man, with Sgt. Stripes, blew a whistle, and the men, turned, and started to hurry off, as Jr. did.

"What's her name," Wilma yelled again.

"Elaine," he said as he was running off with the other troops.

Wilma and Albert stood watching, and Wilma began to sob uncontrollably, and all Albert could do was to hold her, as he cried also.

They kept a close eye on the war, and would every so often receive a letter from him, telling them that he was getting along fine, and his buddies were too. He said they had been pulled back from the line for a rest and thus, he had a chance to write.

He finally admitted, in one of his letters, that he had married a pretty young lady by the name of Elaine Jones, and they had an apartment close to the base, but he thought she might go and move in with her parents, until he came home. He didn't say where her parents lived.

They wrote right away, trying to find out all the particulars on the address of the apartment, her parents name, and where they lived.

Unfortunately, the letter came back unopened, and was simply stamped, "Undeliverable."

Within a day or so, Albert and Wilma were just sitting down to supper, when there came a knock at the door, and Albert went to answer.

There stood an Army Chaplin, an Army Sergeant, and a Lt. Colonel, all with grim looks on their faces. Albert's heart sank, but he invited the men in, and asked them to sit down.

The Lt. Colonel spoke, "Mr. Rogers, we need to speak to you and Mrs. Rogers, if you don't mind."

"Why yes, yes, of course," and he went to the dining room and told Wilma that they had some very important guests she needed to meet also.

She entered the living room, and the three soldiers all stood, and took off their hats, and did not sit down until she did. Then Albert introduced them.

Wilma had a look of bewilderment on her face, but she sat waiting for them to state their business.

The Lt. Colonel introduced himself, introduced the Chaplin and Sergeant, and then opened his brief case and asked, "Are you the parents of one, Corporal Albert Walker Rogers, Jr."

"Yes, we are," answered Albert.

The Lt. Colonel lowered his voice, then said, "I regret to inform you that your son has been reported missing from the field of action, on May 12, 1951. It may be that he is a prisoner of the enemy forces and the Red Cross has not yet obtained his name. If any further information comes available, you will be notified immediately!"

Wilma let out a scream, and Albert rushed to her side, and he thought he heard Annie let out a muffled yell also from the dining room also. Wilma stood up, and then yelled again, "My baby," then fainted.

The Army personnel rushed all over to Albert, trying to assist him if they could, but he waved them off. He yelled for Annie to call the family Doctor.

As he led the Lt. Colonel and his men out, he asked him, "Colonel, confidentially, is there any chance of my son still being alive. I read the newspapers and I know that the Communists don't take too many wounded Allied prisoners, do they?"

The Colonel, sighed, and said, "No sir, they don't. I hate to say this, but if I was you, I would consider him as deceased. I know it's hard to take, but the quicker you realize it, the quicker you can get on with your life."

"Thanks, Colonel, I appreciate your advice, but you see, we have already lost two children, and this one is going to be very, very hard for her to get over!"

The days passed as she really took the news of her son, as if someone had drove a stake through her heart! The loss of the other two children was a very tough time in her life, but she was young and she got over their deaths, fairly quick, but now, she was young no more. She could not have any more children, no, Jr. was the last one, and now, he was gone.

The family Doctor treated her as best he could, but still she was in a state of mild shock. He prescribed what medications that was available at that time, but, they were not helping much at all.

Albert came up with the idea that they would try to find Elaine. This seemed make Wilma a little more responsive as they called and wrote letters to every Mrs. Elaine Rogers or Elaine Jones they could find. But no luck!

Wilma, then lapsed into a deeper state of depression than before. The Doctor prescribed a new medication that had just came on the market, but he warned that she was not to take more than prescribed!

It seemed to help, and Albert again, thought she was getting better. So one morning he came home early, maybe to have breakfast with her.

When he walked into their bedroom, he knew, at a glance, she had found the hiding place of the new medication, because she was lying there, serene and calm, but deathly white. He bent and felt of her cold face, and he kissed her. He walked over to his old roll top desk and pulled out a drawer, and in that drawer was a .36 caliber pistol, that had been handed down through generation of Rogers's. He was going to give it to Jr. when he came home from Korea.

He walked over to the bed, crawled in bedside the still, cold body of his wife, kissed her one more time, and said, "I'll see you in a few minutes, my love," and then he laid his head on the pillow and stuck the gun to temple and pulled the trigger.

As the loud noise of the pistol was heard, the postman was knocking on the door at the same time. "What was that," he asked himself, "Sounded like a gunshot."

In a few moments, he heard screaming from inside, and knew something was wrong, bad wrong, so he decided to take this special delivery letter back to the Post Office, Little did he know, that it was a special letter from the Department of Defense, stating that Corporal Albert Walker

Rogers, had been exchanged during the P.O.W. exchange after the truce and he would be coming home soon. He was also awarded the Silver Star for bravery in combat. The letter was dated July 3, 1953, exactly two years after being reported being 'missing in action' to his parents.

The Doctor stopped talking for a moment, and Bill wondered if that was all.

But, he was mildly surprised when the Doctor stopped their waitress, Marjorie, and ordered another piece of the peach pie and a tall glass of cold milk.

"Wow," thought Bill, "do I going to have enough money to pay for all this, or am I going to have to see about taking out a loan at the bank!"

When the Doctor had been served, he continued between bites, telling how Albert Rogers, had come back from the war, and was briefly stationed in California, at his old base. He was actually in the hospital, undergoing evaluation tests, but he was very anxious to get out, so he could find Elaine.

He was finally released, with a clean bill of health, and he immediately started searching for Elaine. Someone had told him that when the Army had declared him missing and presumed dead, she grieved something terrible. She was pregnant, and knew that she could not raise her son all by herself.

Then she met a nice young man, a returned Navy veteran, from Korea, that understood her problem, and soon, they were seeing each other often. Then one day, he asked her to marry him, as the Navy was discharging him, and he was headed home.

Elaine agreed, and they were married, and shortly, they left the area. But, where they went, and what was his name, the lady had no idea. Maybe, it was Johnson, or, Jones, or Smith, she wasn't sure. She never thought to ask.

Albert Walker Rogers came back to Rogersville, a war hero, but a somewhat broken man. He had won a great medal, but lost his wife and child. That was worse, to him, that losing his mother and dad. He just let the plantation home, and the grounds and the fields, just about go to waste. He sold some of it off, and kept some of it.

"Chief, I wanted to tell you, there was no Maserati, and there was no warehouse full of televisions, stereos and such. It was just a figment of his imagination," concluded the Doctor.

"Thank you, Doctor," said Bill, "I feel as if I have just been in a high school history class. I certainly thank you for the insight into the gist of the Rogers of Rogersville, and for clearing up two of my cases."

The Doctor gave a low laugh, and said, "Buy my lunch again, and I might solve some more of your cases."

Bill laughed, and said, jokingly, "I don't know if I can afford it or not."

CHAPTER 5

At 10:00 A.M. on the appointed day, Ricky and Rita Roberts, and Pete and Marjorie Edwards, met at the designated convenience store, fueled up their vehicles, and was soon, merrily, on their way to the Monte Rialto Hotel.

Rita was particular glad as she didn't have to worry with customers, food orders, or anything to do with a restaurant, for at least two weeks. Oh, she was happy, they owned the business, because it made them a very good living, but it was so nice to get away, once in a while.

Ricky, on the other hand, was thinking about paying some of their bills that would come due while they were gone. But, he knew his creditors would work it out with him, they had in times past when they had run into rough times.

As they sped down the highway, he glanced over at Rita, and she was humming, following a love song on the radio. She was thrilled to take this vacation and he was glad they could do it.

Right behind them was Pete and Marjorie, and they too were thrilled at this chance of getting away "from it all" for two weeks, to be with each other, and be with very close friends, and to enjoy all the offered luxuries.

Andy and Alma Hale was right behind the others, looking forward to a wonderful time, away from their sometimes, dull and ordinary life. They were riding along, enjoying the landscape, the beautiful homes, and as they rolled along, they also were singing hymns from their church.

John and Ruth Sutton was soon on the road also, headed to what they thought was their 'Shangri-la. They were riding along, singing songs that were popular, way back in the 70' and 80's. . But, little, did they know what was ahead of them, if so, they might turn around, and head for home at a rapid pace!

Chief Bill Freeway was, of course, the last to fuel, and get on the road towards the motel. But, within, an hour or so, he pulled in behind the Suttons, and he followed them all the way to the motel-lodge. When they reached the turnoff road, he noticed how the wooden fence was installed and painted white, and every so often, there was a clump of Crepe Myrtle trees planted. The drive wound around the beautiful trees and hills until, all of a sudden, the large motel, seems to just rise up out of the ground.

Bill parked behind the Suttons under the pavilion at the entrance, and two valets, came out to help him unload his pickup. The same was happening to the Suttons, and they walked into the foyer together.

Bill whistled under his breath, "Wow, what a place," as they walked across the beautiful shiny, floor. There were potted plants spaced all over the foyer, and sofas and chairs.

As they approached the sign-in desk, they noticed off to the right, the large restaurant and lounge, and off to the left was the elevators and a gift shop.

A beautiful young woman welcomed them to the hotel, and said, "My name is Angela. It's so nice to have you. Will you please sig our register". Bill watched as John Sutton signed them in, and as he started to sign himself in, he saw he was the last as, McAndrew, Grayson, Roberts, Hales, and Edwards had all signed in.

Angela asked, "May I have your keys, please?"

John Sutton produced hid key and she handed him a plastic key to room 6000. Bill was nest and his key was to Room number 7000.

Angela waved her hands, and three bellhops ran up and soon they were in the elevators, heading to their rooms. Angela told them, that supper would be available from 6:00 P.M. to 10:00 P.M.

When Bill was finally in his room, he checked it out. It really was two rooms in one, not counting a very large bathroom. There was a sitting room with a wide screen television, a wet bar, and a small refrigerator. It had a sofa, and a recliner, and a armchair. The bedroom had a queen-sized bed, with tables on both sides. There was also another television. It had two large walk in closets, with extra shelving. All in all, it was a pretty swanky place, much too rich for a common ordinary Police Chief to afford.

He called down to the front desk and obtained the room numbers of the Roberts, the Hales and the Edwards. He called them and set up a time for all to meet for supper. They all agreed on a time, so he called again and got the room numbers of McAndrew and Grayson, but when he called them, there was no answer, no matter how many times he called or when.

They all met in the luxurious dining room and ordered a meal fit for s king.

After the waitresses had taken their orders, Bill looked around and asked, "Listen gang, doesn't it make you feel kind of strange to be the only ones here in this gigantic dining room."

Marjorie spoke up, "Yeah, it kinds gives me the creeps."

Pete poked her in the side with his finger and said, "Honey, if this place was jammed packed, you'd feel creepy!"

They all laughed and Rita spoke up in defense of her friend, Marjorie, "It does seem weird, doesn't it. All these empty tables and we're the only ones here."

Alma spoke up then and said, "I'll tell you one thing. When Andy and I get through eating, we're heading straight back to our room!"

Andy looked like he was going to say something, but just then, the servers were there with their orders, so he did not get a chance to speak his mind.

Their meal was delicious, and cooked to a 'perfection'. The desserts seemed to be home made, simply melted in your mouth. Andy desired a third helping, but Alma drew the line on two.

When they finished, they all said good night, at the appropriate floors, and planned to meet for breakfast at 9:00 the next morning.

When Bill opened his room door, he looked around, and had the strange impression that someone had been in his room. He looked in the closet, but nothing was changed, and he looked in the drawers of the dresser, and his socks and underwear seemed to be in place, but then he noticed his pistol. It was backwards, from how he had placed it in the drawer. Being a right-hand person, he laid the pistol on its right side so as if he had to grab it in a hurry, he would not have to turn it around first. But, it was lying on its left side, proof that someone had been in this drawer at least.

He checked the weapon out, but found nothing wrong with it. The gun was still fully loaded and there were no tell-tale marks of anyone trying to molest the inner workings.

Now, why would anyone want to sneak through his under-clothes. Were they looking for my gun, and when they found, then what? Again, Bill's suspicion's, began to arouse about this vacation and the purpose for it. He reminded himself to talk to the others and see if they had any snooping around in their rooms.

The next morning, after breakfast, they had all decided to go to the swimming pool. The women were all wishing to try the olympic sized swimming pool that was on the upper side of the grounds.

So, the valets furnished some golf carts, and away they all went, just like a bunch of teenagers on their first day at camp.

The women, all raced to see who was the first in the gigantic pool, but the men, who had planned to hold back, gathered around a table, with a very large umbrella, to protect them from the sun. As quick as they were seated, a young man rushed up, wanting to take their orders for drinks, coffee or soft drinks. They said no for right now, so he half bowed and left.

Bill started the conversation by telling them of his experience in his room, and then asked, "Did any of you see anything, or find anything out of the ordinary, when you got back to your room?"

Most of them shook their heads, but Pete said, "Of, course, I wasn't even thinking about looking, you know. But, come to think of it, I put my shoes in the closet, when we got here, and I found one of them outside the closet, when I got back to the room. I asked Marjorie if she had moved them and she said no."

Bill asked again, "Have any of you seen Grayson or McAndrew, even once, since we have been here?"

Again, they all shook their heads.

"I tried calling both of them in their rooms last night, several times, and got no answer from either one," said Bill.

"Hey, what's going on around here, "asked Ricky.

"Yeah," chimed Andy, "what is going on around here?"

Pete said, "I don't know, but for Marjorie and myself, we're going to be on our up and up until we find out something."

Bill spoke up, "It's a good idea for us all. It may not be a thing, but you never know."

About that time, the women came running over, and started yelling for the men to go and get their bathing trunks on and join them in the pool. As Rita put it, "It was delicious!"

Bill was very tired when he got back to his room, but the first thing he checked was his pistol.

It was in the right position this time, so it seems no one had been in snooping.

After he had taken a shower, and had settled down to watch the Atlanta Braves baseball game against the New York Mets, his telephone rang.

CHAPTER 6

"Hello", he said, and was surprised to hear a familiar voice on the other end.

"Chief," The voice said, "Matthew Grayson, How are you this evening?"

"Doing just fine, Mr. Grayson, and you?"

"I'm wondering if this fine vacation style living might just be too much for me, you know," he answered.

"Yes, I know," Bill said, "a fellow could get used to this kind of living, and in a hurry, I mean!"

"Ha-ha," laughed Grayson, "say would you feel like meeting me down in the lounge and let me buy you a drink, and let's discuss a few things I want to talk to you about?

"Mr. Grayson," Bill answered, "I'd be glad to meet with you, but I don't drink alcohol, of any kind."

"You know, I really shouldn't either, "he laughed as he said it "it's not really good for any part of the body, only for treating animal sickness and such."

"Where and when do you want to meet, Mr. Grayson, "Bill asked?

"Let's see, it's about 6:45 P.M. now, say 8:00 P.M., will that be all right with you and say, at the lounge. No alcohol will be served."

"Sounds great," answered Bill, "see you then." He hung up and wondered what was all this about? Where has he been? And where was McAndrew, maybe he had the answer.

———————————————————————

At 8:00 P.M., Bill walked into the beautiful lounge just off the main lobby, and Matthew Grayson was already there sitting at a table in the middle of the floor.

He waved for Bill to come on over, and Bill extended his arm and shook the old man's hand. It was still a firm grip.

"Hello, Mr. Grayson, ", he said, "it's so nice to see you again."

"Hello, my boy, "Grayson said, "Sit down and quit calling me Mister. Just call me Matt."

"If that's the way you want it, then that's the way it will be," Bill said.

"Do you want anything," Grayson asked," soda, coffee, or milk?

"No, sir, thank you. To tell you the truth, I'm still full from that delicious supper they serve here."

Grayson laughed, and said. "Yes, I know what you mean. If this doesn't hurry and get over with, I'll probably gain 10-20 pounds!"

"Please don't talk like that. "Bill said," I can't afford to gain any weight. It doesn't look right to

133

have a beer barreled belly Police Chief, you know."

They both laughed at that, and then Bill asked, "Okay, Matt, what's this meeting all about?"

Grayson, shuffled around a little, then pulled his chair closer to the table, leaned forward, and asked Bill, "I heard that you had a mighty unusual case, just before we came on this holiday>"

"Well, as a Police Chief, you always have unusual cases,' he answered.

"Yes, but this was about a man that was found dead in his store I believe, if I am correct," Grayson said, matter-of-factly.

"Yes, we had a man that died, possibly on a Saturday night, after closing, and was not discovered until Monday morning, if that is the case you're asking about," he said.

"Who was the man," asked Grayson, bluntly.

Bill thought for a moment, and asked himself, 'Now why does he want to know?'
He started to tell him, that it was still official police business, when Grayson spoke up.

"Bill, I don't want you to think I am interfering with police work, in any way whatsoever. I am simply curious to find out, that's all, and since I am from Rogersville, I thought you could tell me."

Bill, was wondering why did this man want to know. Is he an 'ambulance-chaser'?
Just what was his interest in this? He finally decided to tell him the facts and see just what played out.

135

"Okay," said Bill, "the owner of the electronics store there in town came from a long line of distinguished relatives. Apparently, as some of the town folks believe, he may have been the last, however, our town Doctor doesn't think so. But that's a different story."

"It all started with a light left on in the back office," and Bill relayed the whole incident to Matthew Grayson.

"Who was the Man," asked Grayson.

"Albert Walker Rogers, the last of a line of Rogers, from way, way back!"

Bill thought he saw Grayson stiffen just a little as he said that, but he couldn't be sure. He also, thought that Grayson had turned a whiter shade, but again, in the dim light, he couldn't be sure.

When Grayson, coughed, then he asked Bill, "why does the Doctor think that he is not the last of a long, long line?"

"It's because of something that Rogers told him, in strictest confidence of course, but since the man is dead, I don't see where it would hurt to tell the story."

Grayson coughed a little again, and said, "No, no, I don't either. Please tell me the rest of the story."

"It seems that our man, Albert Walker Rogers, was a hero in Korea, winning the Silver Star for bravery in combat. It also seems he was a P.O.W., and was presumed dead, and his wife was told everything but, that he was alive. So, she was pregnant, with his child, she met a returned Navy veteran, and he married her and moved off, to unknown places."

"Didn't this Rogers try to find her," asked Grayson.

"Oh, yes, in fact, he spent the family fortune trying his level best, but no luck. It seems they just vanished from off the face of the earth!," he said.

"That is a shame, isn't it, to try and locate your son, and always come up empty handed and she truly was wanting him, if he was alive, mind you, to find her, because she probably never stopped loving him."

"How would you know that," Bill asked, quizzically.

"I guess I've seen too many movies," Grayson answered quickly.

CHAPTER 7

Bill had got back into his room just in time to see the announcers sign off for the night, but was able to switch to the ESPN channel and get the final score.

Satisfied, he sat back down and thought about this evening's chat with Matthew Grayson. It left him with the impression that he had interviewed by a very skilled individual, even though, at the time, he couldn't really tell it.

Why was he so interested in the police case about Roger's and did he see him react when he told him the name. He could have sworn he did, but he couldn't be sure.

He racked his brain his brain as any well trained lawman would do, trying to figure the in's and out of Matthew Grayson and their little chat tonight. What was his game, and where has he been.

He completely forgot to ask him that, and what about McAndrew. He made a mental note to be sure and ask him tomorrow. He had to find some answers and quick. Something was not right. He could feel it in his bones. Maybe, he should leave, but what would happen to the others, his friends. No, he would stick it out with them. He had too!

The next morning, they met, as agreed for breakfast. Bill was late, because he overslept, after having a restless night worrying about what was going on.

He soon realized he wasn't the only one, because Ricky and Rita hadn't come down either. Bill wanted to know if anyone had checked with them this morning, but no one had, so he walked up to the front desk, used the telephone, and rang their room. No answer, even after letting it ring for 7-8 times.

Oh well, he thought, they must be on their way down, and he went back to the table and told the others.

But, when twenty minutes had passed, the Roberts hadn't shown and everyone was getting worried. Bill said that they might have gone back to their room, so he went back to the front desk again, and called. This time, a maid answered, and said, "Hello, this is the maid. May I help you?"

Bill said, "Yes, thank you. May I speak to Mr. or Mrs. Roberts?"

The maid answered, "Speak to whom, sir, I know of no Mr. or Mrs. Roberts!"

Bill asked, and gave her the Roberts room number, and the maid said, "Oh, yes sir, this is the right room number, but I don't know of any Roberts, anywhere in the motel!"

Bill hung up, turned to Angela, the desk clerk and asked, "have the Roberts checked out?"

Angela, looking puzzled, said, "There are no Roberts registered here at this hotel, sir!"

"Don't tell me that," as Bill was getting a little upset, "I was with them all day yesterday, and they are good friends of mine, now where are they?"

Angela quickly turned the guest sign-in book around for Bill to see, and said, "Look for yourself sir, there is no Roberts signed in here, not now or ever has been."

Bill roughly grabbed the register, and sure enough, there were the Edwards, the Hales, Grayson, the Suttons, McAndrew, and his, but no Roberts. He knew he saw their name when he checked in, besides he had already spent time with them.

The others crowded around with a lot of questions, but Angela could not answer them all at one time, so unseen, she reached under the counter and pushed a small button, and in a few moments, a door opened, and a well dressed man emerged, and introduced himself as the General-Manager.

"My name is Timothy McDermott, and I will talk to your representative, if you will select one, we will go into our office and see if we can work out any problems."

This seemed to satisfy them for the moment, and John spoke up, "I think Bill ought to be our spokesman."

"Hear, Hear," said Pete, then, oomph" as Bill elbowed in his side.

"Mr. Freeway will do just fine," said McDermott.

Bill threw up his hands as if in desperation, and Angela let him behind the desk. He followed McDermott into his office, and speaking to the secretary as he passed her desk.

It was a plush office, two large sofas, three overstuffed chairs, bookcases full of books around two of the walls, a door, and a French-style door on the south side.

"Very nice," Bill said, "Very nice, indeed."

"Thank you,", said McDermott, smiling, obviously very proud of his office.

"Would you care for a drink," he asked as Bill looked over some of the titles.

"NO, no I don't indulge in the hard stuff," he said, "I see you must like to read westerns, you seem to have a good collection of Louis La'mour, Zane Grey, and others."

"My La'Mour collection is all in leather. I fancy myself to collect westerns, first issue if I can, "said McDermott proudly.

145

"I don't blame you," answered Bill, "but my salary just barely lets me buy used paperback books at the Goodwill store."

"Okay, let's get down to business," Bill said suddenly, as he sat in front of the very, large desk, "All I want to know, is what happened to the Roberts?"

"Mr. Freeway, don't you realize, as the General Manager of this fine motel-hotel, I know everything that goes on around here, and I assure you, there have never been any Roberts booked in with us. I do not know where you and the others got this idea?"

"Mr. McDermott, let me set you straight on a few things. First off, we may be from a small town, but we are not country-hicks as you may suppose we are. We know what is right from wrong, and we'll fight to the death to uphold that belief. We are not stupid either. We all know that we all came here as a group of winners from Rogersville, to enjoy a vacation, but why we were selected, has been a big mystery. Now, as Police Chief, I am holding you responsible, to tell me where the Roberts have gone, or where they may be, and Heaven help you if any harm has come to them!"

With that, Bill stood, turned, and walked out of the offices, without another word to the foyer, where the others were waiting.

They were all asking questions, so he pointed to the dining room, and when they had sat down, he told them the situation.

"Wow," said Pete, "he actually said that there were no people named Roberts registered here? He might as well have called you a liar, and he's doing the same to us!"

"Yes," said John and Andy, almost in unison, then Andy kept talking, "I don't appreciate being called a liar. I never lie, at least, and know I do."

"What does ne take us for, fools," said Ruth Sutton.

"How can he deny that the Roberts were here," Alma said, as she was slowly shaking her head.

"He's doing it," said Bill, "and with a very straight face. He is an old hand at it, I could tell. He is very cool, and suave."

"Maybe," intertwined Marjorie, "I ought to go in there and threaten to scratch his eyes out!"

148

"Simmer, down, you wild cat," said Pete, "simmer down. We don't want you to get a hold on him."

The others laughed slightly, and as they walked away, Pete growled, grrrrr!

Bill stretched, and turned over. The bed felt mighty good, and he was about to go back to sleep, when his telephone began to ring. He was almost tempted to ignore it, but something told him not too, so he reached out, grabbed the receiver, dropped it, then grabbed it again.

"Hello," he said, in a very sleepy voice,

"Bill, are you awake?

"To tell you the truth, I'm still asleep. You are talking to a recording!"

"Aw, come on Bill, this is serious. Wake up, wake up, this is Pete, I've got some disturbing news!" said Pete, excitedly.

"Okay, what is so disturbing this fine morning," he asked.

"I believe that the Sutton's and the Hale's have disappeared also," said Pete, breathlessly.

Bill shot up straight in bed, "What did you say?"

"I said, I believe that John and Andy and their wives have disappeared. We were supposed to meet for breakfast, at 10:00 sharp this morning, but they never showed by 11:00. So, I went to their rooms, and the maids never heard of them. That's when I decided to call you," said Pete.

"I'm glad you did," answered Bill, "give me 15 minutes, and you and Marjorie come up to my room, and come by the stairs, and don't stop for anyone, understand?"

"Aye, aye, sir," answered Pete, "we will see you there."

Bill jumped out of bed, and jumped into the shower and was fully dressed when a knock came at his door. He put his weapon behind him, and slowly opened the door, and seeing it was Pete and Marjorie, he let them in, and looking up and down the hall, and seeing no one, he shut the door.

Pete looked at the Edwards, and Marjorie looked afraid, and Bill put his arm around her and told her to sit down, that everything was going to be all right now.

He got Pete to repeat the story, and Bill stood up, shaking his head, and said, "Pete, we've got a problem. On the one hand, I think we should try to check out and go home, but on the other, we should not leave all our friends here at the mercy of 'who knows what? Don't you agree?"

Pete looked as if he was trying to make a decision, and said finally, "Bill, if it was just me, I'd say yes, let's stay and find out what' going on, but I have Marjorie to think about!"

With that, Marjorie jumped and said almost vehemently, "Pete Roberts, don't you dare let me stand in the way of find out what happened. Remember, Rita, Alma, and Ruth were my dearest friends also, and I want them back. So, don't you dare count me out!"

"Well, Pete, I guess that settles that, " Bill said, "what we have to do now is make some plans.

Bill looked at his watch, and it was almost 6:00 P.M., and he said, "Hey, I don't know about you two, but I am awfully hungry. I haven't eaten all day."

"But," Pete said, "do we dare show ourselves downstairs?"

"Why not," Bill answered, "it might just put them off guard."

"Let's go eat then," Marjorie jumped up, and headed for the door.

When Bill got back to his room, he noticed a bottle of expensive champagne, nestled in ice, and a small white icing cake sitting on the coffee table in his room.

"Mighty nice of them," he said out loud, but I'm too full for anything else tonight.

He turned on the television, and found the Braves baseball game, stripped to his tee shirt, and shorts, and made himself comfortable and watched the game, then he went to bed, early.

CHAPTER 8

Bill suddenly awoke, as if someone was in his room. He arose slowly from the bed, and searched around the room, but could find no one.

He looked at his watch, it was only 10:30 P.M., and he decided to call Pete and talk to him about what time to meet for breakfast in the morning.

He dialed their room, and let the telephone ring, 7-8 times but, no answer. That's odd, they were going straight to their room. He tried again with the same results.

He quickly dressed, put his pistol in his back waist band, opened the door, and seeing no one in the hall, he eased out into the stairwell, and went down the stairs softly to the floor of the Edwards.

When he got to their room, he knocked softly, and the door opened, and he entered, but no one was there.

He noticed the same type of champagne and cake on their coffee table also, but the cake was partially eaten, and several glasses were gone from the magnum of champagne.

Bill picked up one of the empty glasses, and smelled of the partial contents. He thought he smelled a faint odor of a narcotic, or maybe he was only guessing.

He continued to look around the room and he noticed that the carpet had the imprints of wheels that had been recently rolled across. There were two distinct set of prints. Maybe, wheels of hospital guerneys!

Where would they carry the guerneys? There is no hospital section here at the motel. They would have to transport them away, so that means, from the bottom floor.

He quickly was out the door, went to the elevator, pressed the button, and when the doors opened, he got on, pressed the top floor button, then, quickly jumped off, just in case anyone might be trailing him.

He went down the stairs to the bottom floor, and looked down the hall. There was a double-door exit on the left, near the far end of the corridor, and a door on the right, back towards the elevator from the double-doors.

Seeing no one, he eased out and staying close to the left hand side, he worked his way towards the double-doors, hoping to see what was behind them.

When he reached them, he slightly cracked the door, for a small opening, and he saw at the far end, two gurneys, with apparently bodies on both, at the far end of the room. There was a small light over the two, but it was pitch-black dark between the door and the rear of the room.

Bill started to enter, when he heard voices coming up towards the door from the back of the room. He quickly looked for a place to hide, and ran to the room on the right, tried the door, and it opened, and in he went. It was a supply room. He quickly surveyed the room, saw some large toilet tissue cartons in the rear, and he ducked down behind them just in time as one of the men entered.

He was talking to the other, "I brought my supper. It would do you good to bring yours too, you know, but anyway, I'll be here waiting on you."

Bill heard the door close, and then, a sound of what was a lunch box opening, and soon the sounds of eating, was coming from the man. Bill eased up, and through a crack in the boxes, saw that the voice was that of a Security Guard, about 25 years old, about 140 pounds, a Barney Fyffe type of physique.

Soon, the other Security Guard came in, and Bill saw that he was much older, about 275 pounds, grey at the temples, and about 5 feet, 8 inches tall.

"Are you through with your supper," he asked.

"Let's get on our rounds then." Bill heard the door open and the sound of them moving out and then the door closed. He waited a few minutes, then he got up, and walked to the door and listened.

Satisfied that no one was in the hall, he opened the door slowly, and looked out, and he saw the elevator doors, closing and the light indicating it was moving upwards.

He moved to the double-doors, listened, but no sound, so again, he opened one and looked in. It was still as it was before. Two gurneys, with apparently, a body on each, covered in a white sheet.

He started down towards the gurneys to see who was on them, when he heard voices on the outside, at the large double-door leading to the outside, where there was a loading ramp.

Bill looked around and saw a table to his left, and he quickly squatted down and got behind it, hoping it would give him some semblance of cover in this darkness.

The two men came in off the ramp, and Bill was surprised that they were dressed in all white uniforms, the kind that E.M.T's usually wear.

One of them was complaining, "I wish they would come on, I am not too crazy about this kidnapping, you know."

The other snapped, "Aw, quit jawing. They're paying us enough, a whole lot better than when we used to ride in that ambulance, and you know it!"

"Yeah, I guess so, but I still don't have to like it,' he responded.

The second man said, "I'm going out on the ramp and smoke me a cigarette. Do you want to come with me?"

"I don't know," the other answered, "maybe one of us ought to stay with them."

"Oh, they'll be okay. It'll do us good to get out for a while!"

Bill watched from his hiding place as they opened the doors and went outside. He came out from behind the table, and made his way to the double-doors, and slowly opened one of them to check on the E.M.T.'s. He saw them turn a corner, and disappear, behind the corner.

He quickly ran to the first gurney, unbuckled it, and rolled the sheets back, and there lay Marjorie, her eyes wide, and when she seen Bill, he saw a look of relief, come in them almost immediately.

He unfastened all the belts he could find that had her attached to the gurney, and removed the gag around her mouth, and she was just about to say something, when they heard the voices of the men coming back.

Bill recovered Marjorie, and before he could get back to his hiding place, one of the E.M.T.'s had come in, and the other had gone back for another smoke.

The one that had come in, grabbed Bill, swung him around, and landed a punch upside his right jaw. Bill saw stars for a moment and went down, but was up in a flash, and landed a punch to his opponent's stomach, then one to his jaw. He fell, and Bill thought he was out.

He rushed back to where Marjorie was lying, and assisted her in releasing herself from the gurney. He asked about Pete, and all Marjorie could do was point to the other gurney.

Bill started undoing the straps and belts that was securing Pete, when all of a sudden, he was in an arm-lock, and was being squeezed tightly. The raspy voice whispered in his ear, "I've got you now, and I'm going to squeeze the life out of you!"

Bill thought he was too, because he could not free himself, and he was beginning to see stars, and to drift away, when all of a sudden, there was a big "wham," and he let Bill go and the E.M.T. slowly fell to the floor.

Bill, when he caught his breath, looked, and there stood Marjorie with a bent aluminum bedpan in her hands. She had effectively placed it across the back of the man's head with sufficient force to cause him to take a deep sleep.

Bill said, "Thanks, lady, I thought I was a goner there for a moment."

All Marjorie could say was, "I can't believe I did that!"

They got Pete out of his straps, and Bill told him what his wife had done and he said,

"Marjorie, I'm so proud of you. I Love you so very much!"

Bill said, "C'mon, let's get this fellow on one of the gurneys, and see if we can make a dummy for the other, so maybe they won't miss you and we can get away."

Later, when they had accomplished their plan, they went to the double-doors that lead into the corridor. They had full intentions of heading back to their rooms, but just as they were in the hall, they noticed that the elevator light was showing that the car would soon be at their level.

Bill pushed Pete and Marjorie into the supply room, and they all crouched down behind the toilet tissue boxes.

They heard the men go down the hall, probably the Security Guards, Bill whispered, and they lay still, for about an hour.

When it seemed it was quiet, Bill whispered, and asked, "Just how did you two get in this mess?"

"To tell you the truth, I think it was the champagne that was in our room. It was there when we returned from supper."

"Yes, I had some too, but I didn't drink any. Good thing I didn't!"

"But Bill, I examined the bottle, and the original wrapping was intact, so I thought it was okay to drink," said Pete.

"Did you examine the stopper for any pin pricks?"

"No, I never thought too. Dad-blame, how stupid of me!"

"That's the easy way, and don't feel stupid, 99% of people who get drugged, never think to check the top or stopper!"

"Well, the next thing I knew I was lying, strapped down on that gurney, with a gag in my mouth and a white sheet over my head," said Pete, shakily.

Marjorie echoed what Pete said.

Bill told them about trying to sleep, then getting a bad feeling and deciding to check on them, and that's how it all came about.

Pete whispered, "Well, Bill, I'm sure glad you got worried. I don't know where we were headed for, and I don't want to know."

About that time, Marjorie whispered, "Pete, I'm hungry."

Pete answered, "Okay, I'll call room service and order whatever you want."

"I'm hungry too, and it's certain we cannot call for room service, so let's make our own room service," whispered Bill, excitedly.

"Now, just how are we going to do that," asked Marjorie.

"There's an old adage," he said, "if you can't bring the food to you, you go after the food!"

"Huh," said Pete, "I ain't never ever heard that one."

"Me neither," smiled Bill, I just made it up."

"Bill, here you and Pete are carrying on some fun, while I am slowly dying from hunger," she smiled, "but, what is your plan?"

"I will go to the kitchen and retrieve us something to eat. I'll also try to get enough for breakfast also. How would that suit you?"

"If you can do it, "she said, "you, will be my hero for life!"

"Mine too," echoed Pete.

When Bill had made his way up the stairs to the foyer, he stopped in the shadows, and looked around. The place was dark except a few lamps on the walls, in different places round the room.

When he was sure no one was around, he eased through, trying to stay in the dark spots as much as possible, and when he got to the sign-in desk, he stopped to see if there was any sound coming from the General Manager's office. He heard none, so he moved on into the kitchen, to the big refrigerators across the back wall.

The first he opened was stacked full of nothing but eggs, so having no way to cook, he gently closed the door, and moved to the fourth door, reasoning, that the second and third was probably full of bacon and sausage.

He was correct, the fourth was full of sliced cheese of all kinds and flavors, all types of sliced luncheon meats and on the door, was mayonnaise, mustard, ketchup, and horseradish sauce.

He looked in the backroom leading off of the kitchen and found a nice sized basket and filled it with, cheeses of all kinds, luncheon meats, and now he needed to find bread, drinks and utensils.

He looked into a room next to the kitchen and realized it was a bakery, so he found several loaves of fresh baked bread, some cookies, and several cakes. Of course, he loaded them all in his basket, and he realized it was getting heavy. So, he looked for the cold drinks, and in the refrigerator on the end, it was jam-packed with cartons of milk, lemonade, orangeade, grape juice and bottles of water. He loaded as much as he could carry and started back to the stairwell, and as he started to exit the dining room, he heard voices.

Bill ducked down behind a big, woody plant and listened, and he heard the manager say, "Now, you're sure that the Edwards have been shipped. No mistakes this time?"

"Yes sir, no mistakes this time," said a nervous voice.

When Bill heard that, he wondered if they had found Pete and Marjorie, or did the fakes fool them and they just think they have the Edwards?

The only way to find out is to go to the supply room and find out, and when he was sure that the voices were gone, he eased over to the steps, and started down, taking one slow step at a time. When he reached the bottom, there was no one, so he hurriedly made it to the supply room door, slowly opened it, and went in.

He heard Marjorie almost yell, but in a very loud whisper, "Pete, no, that's Bill."

With that, he heard Pete let out a sigh, and let a broom handle fall to the floor. Pete grabbed him and gave him a hug, and said, "Man, we thought we had lost you. I'm sorry about trying to brain you, but I thought it was that guard coming in again."

Bill asked, "Has he been coming in here often, since I left?"

"Yes, quite a few times," said Marjorie, "he almost caught us last time."

"We're going to have to be more careful, say set watch, to keep our eyes open while the others sleep," said Bill.

"Yes, I agree, but I hope you got us something to eat in those bags, because I am not only hungry, but I am thirsty also, "said Pete.

Bill reached into one of the bags and tossed
Pete a bottle of water, which he shared with
Marjorie first, then he drank.

After they had enjoyed some of the goodies,
and were satisfied, Bill told Pete for him to lay
down with Marjorie, and sleep first, and he would
take the first watch.

Bill, when he was sure that they could not be
seen, grabbed a box, and moved it against the wall
and tried to think this thing out. Why, and how,
and what for? It seemed silly, but if he could get at
least one or two answers, then maybe this might
make sense.

Someone was shaking him, and trying to get
him awake. "All right fellow, wake up! wake up!"

Bill groggily opened his eyes and he was looking straight into the barrel of a .38 special revolver. The 'Barney Fyffe' looking security guard had returned and caught him unawares. He had committed the cardinal sin, he had fallen asleep while on guard duty.

Bill raised his head and looked the guard squarely in the eye, but said nothing, "Mister, just what are you doing down here in this supply room. Are you hiding from someone," he asked.

"Uh no," Bill answered, "I got lost, and scared ,you know, and well, I took shelter in here until the morning, so maybe someone would find me, and lead me back to my room."

"What is your name, and what is your room number." The guard asked.

"My name is William Freeway and my room number is 5000," he said.

The guard pulled a small radio from his pocket and reported everything to a central base control, and they instructed him to bring Mr. Freeway to the General Manager's office right away.

Bill saw that Pete was slowly and quietly, sneaking up with his broomstick to lay the security guard out, but Bill spoke up, "I sure am glad you found me, sir, as I want to meet with the G.M., because, I've got a few things to discuss with him."

When Pete heard that, he lowered the broomstick, and silently moved back behind the boxes.

Bill continued, "You know, this supply room is not a bad place to stay if a person or persons has to lay around for a few days or so, you know, especially, if they have good food, and plenty to drink."

When Pete heard that and understood it, he raised his hand above the boxes and waved, but the security guard only gave him a weird look, and with the pistol, motioned for him to start out the door.

He motioned for the security guard to leave, and when he was gone, he motioned Bill to the chair and said, "Sit down, Mr. Freeway, said Timothy McDermott, the General Manager, "I see we meet again."

"Yes, we do", Bill answered, as sat in the overstuffed chair in front of the large desk once more.

"You know," Bill started the conversation, "you didn't have to have me brought here at gunpoint. I would have come, if you had just asked me too."

"I'm sure you would," smiled Timothy, "but why were you in my supply room of all places, and don't say you were lost."

""Okay, I won't say it if you don't want me too. What do you want me to say?"

"Just the truth, Bill, just the truth, that's all I ask. Surely you can do that can't you," Timothy asked.

Bill raised himself up, and sitting on the edge of his chair, looked Timothy straight in the eyes, spoke sternly, said, "I'll tell you the truth when you start leveling with me and of course, you answer my questions, truthfully."

Timothy looked away, aware of Bill's steely blue eyes, and said, "Mr. Freeway, I must remind you that you are, shall we say, a prisoner of mine, and I do not have to answer your questions, not now or never!"

Bill stood up, and walked to the door, and found it was locked. He then walked over to the French-doors, and they too were locked, so he tried to knock out a pane, but they wouldn't break, or even crack.

He heard Timothy laugh slightly, and he turned around, and Timothy was watching him intently, and smiling ear-to-ear.

"Okay, McDermott, what's your game. I want out of here," said Bill, looking straight at Bill.

Timothy laughed slightly, and said, "Bill, the only way out is over my body, and frankly, I don't think you can do it!"

Bill, to Timothy's surprise, was across the room in a flash, and had pulled Timothy out of his chair and landed a hard right to the side of his head. He fell backwards, back into his desk chair and it turned over.

Bill waited until he got up before trying any more punches, so Timothy arose, shaking his head, and said, "Wow, that was pretty doggone good. You move mighty fast for an old man."

"This old man is going to show you a thing or two," replied Bill.

Timothy smiled, feinted a punch to Bill's head, and Bill fell for it, and then Timothy hit him hard in his stomach, then followed with a short jab to Bill's right side of his jaw. Bill spun around, and hit the floor. That hurt, he thought, this kid knows something about fighting, after all!

Bill slowly pulled himself up, and got into a defensive position, but Timothy said, "Bill. We could go on like this all night, until we are both bloody and beat to a pulp. Is that what you want?"

Bill smiled, and rubbing his stomach and jaw, said, "Not on your tin-type, I don't. Where did you learn to fight like that?"

"Let's just say," Timothy answered, "in the service of one of our Uncle Sam's organizations, and I am not talking about the military either."

"I understand," said Bill, "I certainly understand."

When they had both set back down, Timothy said, "Bill, I want to tell you, that I have been tracking you ever since you left the supply room downstairs. I know you were in the kitchen, and you gathered up enough food to last you for quite a while down there."

"I'm a big eater," Bill answered, smiling, "I enjoy eating, especially at someone else's expense."

Timothy laughed, and said, "You know Bill, I like you, I really like you a lot. It's a shame we don't work on the same side, but that could be arraigned, you know."

"Oh no," Bill said, "I'm happy just where I am, and say, you are beginning to rub off on me too!"

"Bill, it could mean at least 6-figures a year," Timothy said, tantalizingly.

"Whoeee," answered Bill, "that's very tempting, but, no thanks. I'll stay where I'm at."

Timothy looked at his watch and said, "It's 8:30 A.M., and breakfast time, so let me buy you a good meal in the restaurant."

CHAPTER 9

Timothy, after eating breakfast with Bill, walked back to his office, and sat down in his office chair. He, on the way in, told his secretary to hold all his calls. He was a little tired, and he wanted to maybe catch a short nap.

Instead of sleep, however, he started remembering back to when he first started with Uncle Sam. He was recruited right out of the university, and put in their rigorous training program. He also had to learn many foreign languages. His difficulty was the Russian language, but he studied and struggled through.

College was tough, but this was the toughest time of his young life. He could not call home, nor write. If he was caught, he would be discharged immediately, and rumor was, admitted to an insane asylum.

He could only receive letters from home, and these were carefully read and re-read by trained personnel, before they were given to the recruits.

He was trained in the martial arts, in Judo, and Karate. He was an 'Ace' on the shooting range in the pistol and rifle arts.

He was taught Morse code, international Morse code, which was different from American Morse code. How to handle all types of radios, and of course, all kinds of explosives.

He was enjoying the training, but was glad when it was over, so that he might begin to really earn his money, so-to-speak.

It came sooner than he thought it would, and he was ready to go. He received his orders and started to carry them out as planned.

He booked his travel to his destination on a tramp freighter, under a fictitious name.

The name and identification papers were all drawn up by the agency, and he was now a different person.

When he arrived in the small South American country, he went to a small dirty, hotel, checked in, using Spanish at all times. His room only had a bed, and one table, with a stained wash basin, and a small water pitcher.

The bed was a small cot, similar to an Army version, that he had to lay on while in training, but this one was subject to crash to the floor at any time, and the sheet and blanket needed a good washing with a, strong bleach.

Now, he had to locate the subject in question, without raising suspicion. He wandered around the area of the last known address the agency had given him, before he left.

He had a camera, so he acted as if he was a tourist, and he took pictures of the old and new buildings, as he walked along. This way, he could look through the windows without raising suspicions.

The people were very friendly, and the children would crowd around, wanting him to take their picture, and sometimes, he pretended to do so. The kids would push and shove and luckily, one day, there was an argument between two of the bigger boys, and one told the other, "Just because his father is General Martinez, did not give him the right to shove others around!"

That was the name of his subject, and Timothy, didn't show any recognition, but decided to follow the young man home.

He broke up the fight and suggested that each of the boys head home and settle down. They both agreed, and turned, and headed for home.

Timothy waited for a few moments, then, slowly fell in behind the General's son, trying to stay out of his sight, so he would not see him following.

The young lad went two more blocks, went into a two story building. Timothy kept on walking, and as he passed, he saw that the building had an alcove, in which two guards sat, with Mauser 7.92 caliber rifles, at the ready.

He went to the end of the block, crossed the street and came back up the other side. As he slowly walked up the street, and when he got across from the General's building, he stopped, and was in the act of taking a picture, when one of the guards came out and yelled in for him to "Halt, no pictures!"

He lowered the camera, as the guard had his rifle at the ready to shoot, and Timothy had the feeling that he would, so he put the camera in the carrying case. The guard let down his weapon and turned and retreated to his post.

He turned around, and realized that this was an apartment building. He went inside and climbed the stairs to the third floor, hoping there was an empty one available facing the street. He found a door, opened it, and entered an empty apartment, one that faced the General's home. It provided just what he needed, an open view of the front, the windows, and a patio on the side.

He stood back in the shadows, trying to stay hid as much as possible. This was the ideal selection, and hopefully, he could get up here, do his business, and get out, sight unseen.

He went back to his hotel, repacked his bag, and sneaked out the back way, and worked his way to the empty apartment. He unloaded his special brief-case, and there was a .343 rifle with a scope attached, and a clip with eight bullets, all hollow point.

The bullets are designed to kill, and when they strike their victim, they tend to explode, and cause considerable damage to the intended victim.

He assembled the rifle, loaded it, removed the lens cap, then put on plastic gloves, and took the oiled rag, and wiped the weapon down, thus removing all the fingerprints.

Now, all he had to do was wait. He sat back in the shadows, and one time, he heard footsteps, and talking on the stairs, and he was ready to shoot if they came in, but the voices turned and went elsewhere.

Soon, the sun was gone, and someone lit some torches on the patio, and a table was set.

He heard a slight commotion in the street, and he eased forward and peeked over the window sill, and saw that a Lincoln limousine had just pulled up at the General's door and two guards stood at the backdoor. A medium built man emerged, with a uniform that behooves a General, saluted the men, and hurriedly, entered the building.

"Well, well," thought Timothy, "the mighty man is home at last."

Timothy could see by the shadows that he was welcomed home by his family and he had pangs of regret, knowing he was fixing to take their father and husband away from them, but from what he had read about the General, he had no qualms about slaughtering family members at will.

He rechecked the rifle, and was satisfied that everything was okay, knew he must wait for the most opportune shot." One shot, one kill," that was the motto, at the sniper school of the agency, and he was hoping he could live up to it.

Soon, the family was eating on the patio, and he knew he couldn't dare take a shot, even though, he had a clear shot.

Soon, the family was through, and the General had lain back, with a cigar and a glass of wine, and was sitting there, all by himself. It was now or never!

He aligned the General's head with the cross-hairs in the scope and almost squeezing the trigger, when he saw movement. Apparently, his wife had come back to bring him more wine. Then she went back into the house.

Again, he sighted on the General's head, and this time, he fully squeezed the trigger, and felt the rifle kick back. He kept the scope on the General's head and saw the forehead disappear in a flash of gore. That was all he needed. He laid the rifle down, and was out the door and down the steps quietly, within a matter of seconds.

He made it to the airport, caught his flight and returned to Washington, where he was congratulated by all of his supervisors. He saw on the late news that night where an unknown assassin had killed the General. There were no leads, and it was thought that a rebel band member had done the shooting.

He returned to duty almost immediately, and was assigned a desk job, which was boring, boring, but he figured that sooner or later something would come his way.

One day after work, as he was walking to his automobile, his cell phone rang. He answered and it was his Grandfather, "Hey, son. Where are you? I've been trying to get in touch with you all day!"

"Grandfather, it's good to hear your voice," answered Timothy, "but, the reason I didn't answer is because I have to turn my cell in when I walk in the building, and cannot have access to it until I leave."

"Oh, well," said the gruff voice, "That answers that. Where are you right now?"

"I'm standing right in front of the building."

"Don't move, we'll pick you up in just a few minutes," his Grandfather said.

Once Timothy was in the Cadillac limousine, and they were meshing with the late Washington traffic, Grandfather asked him point blank, "Timothy, just how much do you make in a year?"

Timothy told him, and then Grandfather told him, "I want you to come to work for me. I will triple your salary, all expenses paid, and I will furnish you a new automobile, again, all expenses paid."

Timothy could only hold his breath for a moment, trying to let what his Grandfather had said sink in. "But, the agency will not let me go. I have to give a year's notice!"

Grandfather, patted him on the knee, and said, "Maybe the man we're going to see can help us. Maybe he can get that time reduced quite a bit."

At that time, they pulled into the drive of the White House, and after the driver had shown the guards the appropriate passes, they were shown through, and they pulled up to a side door.

They entered, and soon, his Grandfather motioned for him to sit at a small table and to wait, and he was escorted down the hall, and disappeared through a side door. Timothy looked up and down the hall, paying special attention to the walls, and the paintings hanging on them. He wondered just how many years they had been hanging there. Had Mrs. Teddy Roosevelt purchased the paintings, or do they go back further than that?

Soon, the door at the end of the hall opened, and his Grandfather emerged, and shortly, they were pulling out of the White House drive onto Pennsylvania Avenue.

"Grandfather, I didn't know you knew the President of the United States," said Timothy, admiringly.

"Oh yes, my son, I have known him ever since he was on the ranch down in Texas," was the reply.

"You know, old man," said Timothy, "you always seem to amaze me."

"Now," said the old man," let's go by and pick up your old car, and take it to your apartment, leave it, and go somewhere to eat, what do you say to that?"

"Suits me," was Timothy's reply.

While they were eating at one of the finest restaurants in Washington, and several distinguished people, not counting many influential senators, Grandfather made the following remark, "When are you ready to start working for me, son?"

"Grandfather, I've already told you about the agency," he replied.

"Do you remember the man we went to see, in that big white house," asked the Grandfather.

"Yes, so what, Grandfather," asked Timothy.

"That man, as a favor to me, has already got you released from that commitment, so don't worry, you're already on my payroll!"

Bill moved in his chair. That was a very interesting story, and he told Timothy so. "Timothy," he said, "I am led to believe that the agency was the C.I.A."

Timothy smiled and said, "You know the old saying, 'If I tell you, I'd have to kill you!"

Bill laughed and said, "I bet you would too, I bet you just would."

Timothy asked, "Bill why don't you reconsider about my offer. At least, don't say no today, think it over, and let me know before you and the Edwards leave for Rogersville."

Bill sat up, mildly surprised, "You mean that we are free to go?"

"Why, yes of course," Timothy answered, "You can leave at any time. By the way, I've already escorted had the Edwards from the supply room to their room they were assigned, and you are welcome to go to yours now, if you like."

Bill stood up, still not knowing what to expect, said, "Yes. I would like to very much. I need to shave, shower and lay down for a while, if that's okay with you?"

Timothy didn't say anything, just waved his hand and smiled, as Bill exited the office, and made it up to his room. He immediately called Pete, and yes, they were okay, and Bill told them they could leave whenever they were ready.

After a shave and shower, Bill crawled into bed, and was soon fast asleep. He did not hear the maids as they entered his room, gathered his dirty clothes, and silently, left the room. He didn't hear them, when they returned with his clean clothes, either.

CHAPTER 10

The next morning, Bill, Pete and Marjorie decided to head for home, so they requested their vehicles be brought around.

They checked out, and, soon, were on their way to Rogersville, with Bill following Pete and Marjorie.

When they arrived in town, Pete waved at him as they turned to go to their home, but Bill, decided to go by Police Headquarters, and see what was happening in Rogersville.

He walked down the hall, identifying himself so as not to scare Rosie, like he did before. "Rosie," he called out, "Rosie, it's me. Bill."

"Chief, I'm so glad you're back. I'm glad to see you, "she said excitedly.

"It's so good to be back," he said, "what has been going on since I've been gone?"

"Not much of anything," said Rosie, "but how was your vacation?

"If that is what you want to call it," answered Bill, "it wasn't all it was cracked up to be!"

Rosie looked bewildered, and asked, "Well, come on, tell me, I'm waiting for you to tell me what happened."

"Rosie, I lost some good friends of mine while we were supposed to be enjoying ourselves, but in reality, it was a horrible nightmare for some."

"That doesn't sound too good Chief, especially about losing some people. How did you manage to do that," she asked.

"It wasn't easy as you might think, Bill said, sorrowful, "I lost the Hales, Roberts, and the Suttons. Believe me, when I say I lost them, I really lost them.

Rosie could only stand there, wanting to ask a dozen questions, but not knowing where to start, so she slowly sat back down.

"Rosie," Bill continued, "I know by the look on your face, you are totally confused, and I don't blame you. Those people, were there one day, and gone the next. They disappeared from the motel, and what's more, there is no record of them ever being there."

Rosie asked, "But, Chief, didn't you see them while you were up there?"

"Oh yes, several times. We ate together, and we enjoyed the amenities they offered, so it doesn't make sense, as to why they suddenly disappear!"

"Do you have any idea where they may be," asked Rosie.

"At this time, the answer is no," said the Chief, "so I decided to come back and try to pick up some leads from here."

Bill turned to go and said to Rosie, "Please don't tell anyone what I just told you for right now. I'd like to keep it a secret."

Rosie nodded, and Bill said as he walked out of the room, "I'm officially on duty now, so please enter that in your log. Also, I'm heading to the house to get a good night's sleep!"

Rosie said okay Chief, and as Bill walked out of the building, he noticed a white Dodge charger sitting across the street. He noticed it because he personally liked the sleek design of that model, and was hoping he could persuade the City Council to purchase them so as to replace all the worn-out patrol cars they were now driving.

He backed out, and was on his way home when he saw the Charger behind him, and it seemed as if it was following him. He made several unneeded turns just to see if it really was, and it followed him every time.

He sped up, whirled down an alley, and came to an abrupt stop and jumped out of his truck, and waited for the automobile to follow him, but he was disappointed when he saw the Charger hurry

208

by on down the street. He thought about following, but knew that by the time he backed out, and turned, the car would be gone, so he just headed for home.

The next morning, he decided to call Pete and Marjorie at home to see if everything was okay when they arrived there. He let the telephone ring and ring, but no answer.

That worried him, but what was he to do, and he decided to go to their home, and as he started to turn, he noticed that the restaurant that Ricky and Rita Roberts owned, was open for business.

He drove into a parking place and hurried into the restaurant, fully expecting to see the smiling face of Ricky Roberts, but when he entered, all he saw was Marjorie Edwards, running like crazy, waiting on tables.

Bill stood there for a moment, looked for an empty table, spotted one near the back, and headed for it, speaking to several people as he went.

Marjorie saw him and headed straight to his table, and asked, "Bill, do you want some breakfast?"

Bill looked at the menu, ordered, and started to ask her some questions, but she said, as if anticipating what he was going to ask, "This crowd will soon slow down and I can sit down and talk, okay?"

All Bill could do was nod in the affirmative, and Marjorie was gone.

Later, as Bill was sitting there, and having finished his breakfast, Marjorie came over and sat down, and said, "Bill, would you believe. I no more than got home, than I got a call from Larry Roberts, who is Ricky's nephew, and he was going to open up this morning, and wanted me to come in and serve as a waitress."

Bill looked at her, and she looked tired, "I was mighty disappointed when I didn't see Ricky or Rita in here."

"I believe it would have been a lot better knowing they were here to operate this restaurant," she said wistfully, "I miss Rita."

"Who is this nephew of Ricky," asked Bill, "and what do you know about him?"

"Not much," she answered, "only that Ricky supposedly called him, told him where the keys were, how to pay the bills, where the money was, and all that stuff."

"He said that Ricky called him!"

"Yes, that is what he told me," she answered, say, why don't I introduce you to him?"

"That's fine with me," he said, "I think I need to talk to him."

"My name is Larry Roberts," the young man said, as he stuck out his hand, "I am Ricky's nephew, and I am from Virginia Beach, Virginia."

The Chief shook his hand and said, "When did Ricky call you and ask you to open his restaurant?"

"Well, to tell you the truth, he didn't exactly call me, Chief," said Larry.

"Oh, then how did you get the directions to open up?"

"Chief, what I meant was, he left all the information on my answering machine, and I just simply followed his orders. Ricky is my favorite uncle, you know!"

Bill asked, "I assume you still have a copy of this recording."

Larry shook his head and said, "No Chief, I'm sorry, it was a case of another message getting recorded over Ricky's message. Again, I'm sorry."

Bill eyed him suspiciously, and decided that something wasn't right. He was just too convenient for Bill's way of thinking.

He paid his tab, left Marjorie a tip and headed back to his office and when he got back to his office, he called a certain number, and a gruff voice answered.

Bill told him he would like a check run on Larry Roberts, of Virginia Beach, Virginia. He wanted to know everything there was to know about him. The gruff voice said he would get back in touch as quick as he found out anything.

He stayed in the office, waiting on the telephone call, and while he was waiting, he caught up on his paper work. He had his lunch brought in as he was afraid there might be a call, and he wouldn't be there to answer it.

At 3:45 P.M., the telephone rang, and it was the gruff voice, "Bill, are you sure that you have the right name and address?"

"That's all I have on him right now," Bill answered.

"It's not enough," said gruff voice, "we have been trying to find out anything in the whole state of Virginia about a Larry or Lawrence Roberts, and we can only come up with a Southern Baptist Minister, in Richmond."

"So, you're telling me, that this is a fake name, and address, aren't you?"

"Exactly, my boy, exactly," said gruff voice, "he's as fake as a three dollar bill. Can you get me something else, say fingerprints, or a picture?"

"I will certainly try," he said, "and I will fax them to you, ASAP!"

"Good boy," said gruff voice, "just get me something to work with, then we'll nab this faker, if he is one!"

Bill continued working in his office and not realizing the time, until Rosie came in a 6:00 P.M., for her nightly shift, did he decide to call it a day.

He told Rosie "Good Night," and walked out the front door, and that is when he spied another white Charger, parked across from the office.

He reentered the building, went to the dispatch room, told Rosie of his plan, and then went out a back door, and crossed the street, and hunched down, and moved slowly to the back of the Charger.

He stopped, and peered through the back window. There seemed to be only one occupant, that he could see, so he slowly worked his way to the front door, driver's side, and hoping beyond hope, that the door wasn't locked, he quickly grabbed the handle, and luck was with him, as he flung the door open and said, very sternly, "Okay, who are you, and what are you doing spying on me and the police department?"

A feminine voice came back, "I wasn't spying on the police department."

Bill said, "I'm the Police Chief, and I'm ordering you to get out of the car, and keep your hands where I can see them."

The female slowly, slid over and exited the car and with her hands held high, said, "Why are you doing this, I haven't broken any laws, have I?"

Bill answered her in a gruff voice, "Someone, in a car, just like yours, was following me, and I suspect, to do me bodily harm, and I want to know why!"

"It couldn't have been me, I just got into town this afternoon," she said, almost crying.

"What's your name?"

"Mary Josephine Knowles," she answered, "of Montgomery."

"Okay, Miss Knowles, let's go over to the station, I would like to question you a little further," he said,

"Can I put my hands down," she asked.

"Yes, but remember, no funny stuff," Bill said.

Bill had her show him some identification and her driver's license indicated that she was telling the truth about her name and where she was from.

So Bill asked her why was she in Rogersville, and why was she asleep in her car?

She replied, "I heard that you had an opening for a patrolman, and I want to put in an application for the position, when you opened in the morning."

Rosie came and was standing at the door, looking and listening, as to what was being said,

219

and Bill asked Mary, "Why don't you get a room at the Sandy motel, instead of sleeping in your car?"

Mary looked a little sheepish, and said, "To tell you the truth, Chief, I just don't have the money to stay in a motel, because if you turn me down, I have just enough cash to buy gas to get back home."

The Chief looked up at Rosie and asked, "Do we now have or do we expect any visitor's tonight?"

Rosie thought for a moment, then, said, "I don't think so, Chief. The mill doesn't pay until next Friday, so I don't think we'll have any visitor's at all."

Bill looked at Mary, and asked, "We have a nice clean jail, with new beds, and linen, and you're welcome to stay tonight in one of our cells. No harm will come to you, at least, not a larger chance as you sleeping in your car."

Mary thought for a moment, then said, "That's awfully kind of y'all, Chief, and I sure appreciate you helping me this way."

The next morning, Bill decided to come in early, real early, before Rosie's shift ended. He walked into the dispatch office, but there was no Rosie there.

He entered the steps leading down to the jail cells, and when he got almost to the bottom, he saw blood on the last three steps. He drew his pistol, and slowly entered the room where the jail cells were located.

He heard voices, and silently worked his way, to where the sound was coming from. He saw Mary standing over a form who was lying on the bed. Maybe, it was Rosie.

He pointed his pistol at Mary, jumped out of the dark, and yelled, "Okay, just hold it right there. Don't move!"

Mary froze, and from the bed, Rosie said, "Chief, put that thing away before you hurt someone!"

"Rosie," he asked, "you okay."

"Of course, thanks to Mary," she answered.

Bill felt foolish now as he holstered his weapon, asked, "What happened?"

Mary spoke up and said, "Rosie was coming down the stairs and she tripped, hit her head, and that's where the blood came from!"

"Bill looked down at Rosie, and asked, "Do you need to go to the E.R. or to a Doctor?"

"No, sir," Rosie answered, and rose off of the cot, "But, I would like to go home, if it's alright with you Chief."

"Of course, it is, can you make it up the stairs," he asked.

"Yes sir, I think I can," she said, and started for the stairs, with Mary and the Chief right behind her. There came a sound from up the stairs, as Jimmy came in for work, and heard the commotion in the cells.

The Chief told Jimmy that he was taking Rosie home, and then told him why. He asked Mary to accompany him, as he might need her, just in case,

When they arrived at Rosie's home, a small white house with a screened in porch, she and the chief got out of the patrol car, and a slightly grey older black woman came out to meet them, and seeing the bandage on Rosie's head, began to fuss, "Rosie, I told you.! Police work was gonna get you hurt, someday!"

"Chief, this is my mother, Mrs. Melton, and Mom, this is Chief Freeway."

"Pleased to meet you, Chief," her mother said.

The Chief answered, "The pleasure is all mine. Say Rosie, you didn't tell me you had such a fine looking young lady for a mother."

With that, Rosie's mother's attitude changed from a sour look to a big smile, and asked, "What happened to you, girl?"

"I just slipped and fell and the Chief was kind enough to bring me home, that's all," answered Rosie.

"Mrs. Melton, if you can take over from here, I'll be heading back to work, and Rosie, if you can't come into work tonight, let me know, and we'll get your relief to set in for you."

"Okay, thanks Chief, I will, answered Rosie, as she and her Mom started inside. He heard her Mom say, "Why Rosie, he's so nice!"

Bill smiled, and when he got back to his car, he got Mary to move up front with him, and he asked her if she was hungry. She said yes, and they were on the way to the restaurant.

On the way, Bill told Mary, that he indeed, needed another Patrolman, but he had to run it by the City Council. He was almost sure they would approve it, but his hands were tied, until then. However, he knew where he might get her a fairly good paying job, if she really wanted to work. She said that she did.

When they had finished eating, most of the crowd had thinned out and Larry came out of the kitchen, and Bill waved him over to their table.

Larry stood there, and after shaking hands with the Bill, Bill introduced him to Mary, and said that she was looking for a job. Larry looked at her, then, asked, "Have you ever done waitress work before?"

"Yes, but it was way back in high school," she replied.

"Can you report at 5:00 A.M. in the morning, and every morning, Monday through Friday, and your off days will be Saturday and Sunday," he asked.

"Yes, yes, I can," she answered, "but do I need a uniform, or just everyday clothes?"

Larry looked towards the back as Marjorie came out from the kitchen, and Larry called her over. "Marjorie, this is Mary Jo Knowles, and she's starting in the morning, so show her around, will you. Thanks"

Mary Jo walked off with Marjorie, and Bill uttered his "Thanks," and went to the cash register to pay his bill, but Larry refused to allow him to pay.

Bill made his way back to his office, after making a cruise throughout the downtown area, trying to catch speeders, or look for suspicious loiterers. Seeing neither, he sat down at his desk, and the telephone rang and it was the gruff voice he was so use to, "Hey, bud, have you got the information I need to find out about this fella yet?"

"Nope, not yet, in fact, I've been busy with another matter and just haven't had time, but I'm working on it," said Bill.

"Well, just keep me informed," said the gruff voice, and he abruptly hung up.

"That's just like that old walrus," muttered Bill, as he hung up.

About 3:00 P.M., Mary Jo came bounding in his office and told him she appreciated him getting her the job, and introducing her to Marjorie, because she also got her a room at a Mrs. Blackwell's home. Mrs. Blackwell usually didn't rent out rooms, but she knew Marjorie real well, and she seemed to like Mary Jo, so she rented her a room with a bath.

Bill was glad, and he, out of the blue sky, and before he could stop himself, asked if she would like to ride up to Clinton, to the Steakhouse, for supper tonight. She jumped at the chance, and the date was set for 7:00 P.M.

CHAPTER 11

The next morning as Bill was sitting in his office reviewing and signing papers, he thought about the date that he had with Mary Jo, the night before.

He was nervous, and he told her so. He told her just how long it had been since he had been on a date, and all about his dead wife. She, listened, taking it all in, as if she was very interested, and if she wasn't, she certainly put on a good show.

He must get back to concentrating on the missing people from Rogersville. He had to solve whatever happened to them, and pray that nothing harmful has happened to them. But, why these people? There is a connection, and it's got to start here, but where and with who?

Maybe, he should go to the county seat, and check through courthouse records, but where would he start? Should he check with the County Sheriff's office and see if they had any idea? He decided it was a good a place as any to begin, so he decided to make a trip to see the Sheriff tomorrow morning.

He looked in telephone log, and dialed the sheriff's number and asked the Sheriff if he could meet with him, say around 8:00 in the morning?

The sheriff said, why sure, to come on up, that he would be in his office until at least noon.

At lunch time, Bill went to the restaurant to eat, and he sat where Mary Jo would have to wait on him. After he ordered, she brought his plate, and stood for a moment, then said, "I really enjoyed last night."

He looked up, and smiled, "I truly did too. It's the most fun I've had in a long, long time." She smiled, and turned to other tables.

In a few moments, she was back, just as he was finishing, and she asked, "Are you coming in tomorrow morning for breakfast?"

"No," he answered, "I have an appointment with the Sheriff. We're going to talk about the disappearances of some of the people from this town."

"Oh," she said, "I've heard about that. Several of the customers were talking about it. It's mighty strange, mighty strange, isn't it?"

"Yes, and it was done right under my nose, so to speak, but I will get to the bottom of it, if it takes the rest of my life," he said.

"If you need any help, just look towards me, and whistle, and I'll come running," she laughed lightly.

Bill laughed slightly, eyed her, and said, "Believe me, when I do, they'll be able to hear my whistle all the way to Montgomery!"

The next morning, after Bill had checked in his office, reviewed the dispatcher's log, and seeing no extra than normal activity, told Jimmy that he was going to Clinton, to the Sheriff's office.

It was a nice fall morning, the temperature was in the low 70's, and the sun was showing brightly through broken clouds.

Bill had just put on his sunglasses, when there was a loud explosion, and glass flew all over his neck and in the front seat of the automobile. Luckily, there was no other car coming as he would have certainly hit them head on, as the sound made him jump, and he inadvertently, snatched the steering the wheel, and the car wheeled to the left.

He speeded up until he found a side road, pulled off, and jumped out, and inspected the damage. The back window behind the driver's side was completely blown away!

He looked in the front and back, trying to see if he could locate the bullet. He found it, down in the back of the headrest on the passenger's seat. He took his pocketknife, extracted it, and examined it and determined it to be, probably, a .30-06 or somewhere close to that.

Someone had tried to kill him, or had they? Maybe, they were just trying to scare him off? He had been shot at before, during his many years with the State Troopers and the Alabama Bureau of Investigation, so it was nothing new.

Still, it unnerved him. No one enjoyed being shot at, and if he said he did, he was either a liar or a fool!

So, he now knew that he had ruffled the feathers of someone concerning the disappearances of the townspeople. Someone who knew he was going to see the Sheriff this morning, and he had only told two people, Jimmy, the dispatcher, and Mary Jo.

He would question both when he got back to Rogersville, and he would find out the truth!

When he arrived at the Sheriff's office, he reported to the Sheriff, and introduced himself. The Sheriff, a tall man, about 6" 3", and physically, well built, stuck out his hand and said, "It's a pleasure to meet you Chief. My name is

Walter Pierson. I've been Sheriff of this county for about 30 years no. I've been planning on coming down to meet you, but I've been real busy here lately, and just haven't had the chance."

"That's okay, Sheriff," Bill said, as they sat down in the Sheriff's office, "I know what you mean. It seems that there is never enough hours in the day, does it?"

"No, it doesn't," said the Sheriff, "seems that drugs is getting the upper hand some times, and of course, moonshine is still being made in this county too, you know."

"No, I didn't, but I'll be sure to look for it down our way," said Bill, "but you know I have a great problem hanging over my head, and I truthfully don't know where to start!"

"Yes, I've heard," said the Sheriff, "and I don't envy you whatsoever. Can you tell me what really happened?"

Bill started at the beginning, and told him the whole story, even down to the story of Timothy McDermott.

The Sheriff looked puzzled, and asked, "Why, on this green earth did he let you and the Edwards go free?"

"That is the $64,000 question," answered Bill, "that's another angle that's about to drive me crazy."

"Well, I'll tell you Bill," the Sheriff said slowly, "it's been my experience that there's one of two things, or maybe both, that causes a mystery like this, and that's number one, money

238

and number two, is land. People will kill for these two, and for both together, there is no telling what they would do!"

"So, you're suggesting that maybe I should start looking for either of these two, or maybe both, and I might be able to unravel this mystery," said Bill.

"Yes, I am," said the Sheriff, and he turned and pointing to a map of the county that was on the wall behind his desk, continued, "I, if I was you, would probably start right here with this property."

Bill got up and walked behind the desk, and the place that the Sheriff was pointing to was the old Rogers Plantation, faintly outlined on his county map.

"Why that property?" asked Bill.

"No particular reason, but you've got to start somewhere. Go to the county courthouse and see if there has been any recent activity going on concerning that property."

Bill thanked the Sheriff, and could have kicked himself as he walked out of his office. Why didn't he think of that?

He decided to eat lunch with Mary Jo, after he grilled Jimmy and was satisfied he had told no one, about his trip to the Sheriff's office. So, that left Mary Jo.

The usual lunch crowd was all but gone when he walked in to eat. Mary Jo met, all smiles, and she led him to one of her tables, and took his order.

He asked her to sit, when she brought his plate, and he slowly, asked her if she had worked all this morning.

She looked surprised, then answered, "Why, yes, yes I have. I've been here straight since 5 this morning. Why?"

"Just wondering, that's all," he said, but did you tell anyone I was going to the Sheriff's office this morning?"

"No, I didn't, at least I don't think I have," she answered.

"Well, think hard, it's very important."

"Let's see. Oh, wait a minute, Larry asked me if you were coming in this morning, and I think I told him you were going up to Clinton to see the Sheriff. Why? Did I do something wrong?"

"Maybe not, let me ask you another question. Did he leave for any extended amount of time," Bill asked.

"Yes, he went to the bank, at least that is where he said he was going, and he left us with a house full, he did!"

"Thanks, Mary Jo, say, we on for tonight?"

"Just name the time, Big Boy, just name the time,"

CHAPTER 12

Bill had some thinking to do so he drove up the county road to the road that led to the old Plantation home. He noticed that someone had driven straight through the police tape. He turned around and entered the road, stopped, got out and examined the tire tracks. They were an unusual tread type. He quickly pulled out his pad and pencil, and tried to draw the pattern as best as he could.

He had suspicions as to who owned the vehicle, that had these tires, but he had no proof, as yet, but he will get it. If it was true, why was he here, and what was he looking for?

On the way back to town, he received a call from Jimmy, the dispatcher, and he answered.

"Go ahead, Jimmy, this is the Chief."

"Chief, Robert has stopped a vehicle up on Alabama Highway Number 121, north of

Rogersville, and the man said, he wants to talk to you, personally."

"10-4, Jimmy, tell Robert to hang on and I'll be there in a few minutes!"

Bill pushed down on the accelerator, and the new Dodge Charger, Police Special, jumped and was speeding down the highway at a very easy clip. He reached down and turned on the blue light, and siren.

As he was speeding along, he was certainly glad that they had seen his view and bought seven new Dodge Chargers, so that the young, hot rods around the town could not out run his men any more, and then meet at the hangouts, and brag about it.

He soon saw the blue lights of Robert's patrol car, and he stopped his siren and blue lights, and coasted in front of the new limousine.

He hopped out of his car, and Robert was coming forward to meet him, when Bill said, "No Robert, stay with your man. I know him, he's really dangerous!"

With that, Robert turned as if he was catching his man in a silent attack.

The man laughed, and so did Bill, who stuck out his hand and shook the hand of Timothy McDermott.

Robert looked completely confused, as one minute ago, the Chief was practically telling him that this was a ferocious man, maybe a serial cop killer, but now, they are shaking hands and laughing.

Bill saw the confusion in Robert's face and said, "Robert, I'm sorry if I have confused you. This is Timothy McDermott, the manager of the luxurious Monte Rialto hotel up in North Alabama."

Robert slowly held out his hand and in a lackluster way, shook Timothy's hand. He then turned to the Chief, and said, "Chief, if you don't need me anymore, I'm going back on patrol duty."

"That's a good idea," said Bill, "and Robert, you did a mighty good job!"

Robert bowed his head, just a little, and then was in his patrol car and was gone, as Bill and Timothy walked up to Bill's patrol car,

Bill asked, "Timothy, what in the world are doing down here?"

"To tell you the truth, it's on business, but it wasn't in Rogersville, it was in Selma," he said.

"In Selma," Bill asked.

"Yes," Timothy answered, "we had a patron that came up and stayed a week with us, and we unfortunately, took a check in payment, and it bounced higher than the motel, so I had to go and collect."

"Have any trouble," Bill asked.

"No," Timothy answered, "I laid the law down to him and he came across, and he also wanted to pay for my expenses for collecting the money. He was scared!"

Bill laughed, and said, "I would have been too, if you had laid the law down to me too!"

"Well, let's hope that never happens, Bill. Say, have you given any more thought to the offer I made you?"

"Truthfully, no I haven't. I've been too busy, to think about much of anything."

Timothy said thoughtfully, "I've got to be going, Bill. My grandfather is not doing too well here lately. He's so hard headed, he will not listen to his Doctors or take his medicine, and I'm scared every time the telephone rings, that someone is going to tell me that he is gone, you know?"

Bill asked, "You're pretty close to your Grandpa, aren't you?"

"Yes, when my Mother and Father were killed in the plane crash, he and my Grandmother, took me in, and raised me. My Grandmother died several years ago, and we have relied on each other, for comfort, and consolation, when either needs it."

Bill reached across Timothy and opened the door, and said, "Get out of here, before I arrest you for loitering. Get out of my jurisdiction, and make it quick!"

Timothy grabbed Bill's hand, shook it, and said, "Thanks Bill, I'm on the way," and with that he was out and gone.

Bill watched the limousine disappear up the highway, and he turned and headed back to town. He was stopped at a stop sign and a pickup came by, and Larry Roberts was driving. The pickup had mud all over the wheel wells, and on the fenders. Bill watched him go by, and decided to give him about a ten minute head start and then follow him to his apartment.

This he did, and he slowly passed by the apartment building, and he spotted Larry's pickup. He assumed Larry had already entered into his apartment, so he went down the street, and turned around, and came back, and stopped behind Larry's pickup.

He got out and examined the truck, the tires, and he matched the tread against his drawing and it matched. The mud was similar or an exact match to mud at the Plantation site.

He didn't notice, being so involved in his examinations, that had Larry walked up.

"Just what do you think you are doing," asked Larry, rather roughly?

"I'm doing police work," was the only answer Bill could come up with in a hurry.

"Why, police work with my vehicle, I'd like to know?

"To tell the truth, I'm doing some investigating that's quite private at this time, however, I'll be glad to tell you, when I can," Bill answered.

Bill casually walked back to his patrol car and drove off, with Larry standing there, with his hands on his hips and staring at the Chief.

The next morning, as Bill was eating his breakfast, Larry stopped by his table, and said,

"You and I have got to talk. Meet me here at 5:00 P.M."

"Bill without looking up, said, "I'll be here!"

He went back to his office and was having a hard time concentrating on his work because of two things. One was the meeting with Larry at the restaurant, and the other was about a beautiful, blonde named Mary Josephine Knowles. This, has never happened to him before, Since his wife had died, he hadn't hardly looked at another woman, but this lady was beginning to take up a lot of his free thought time, and he wondered just where it would lead.

He thought and felt positive, that a woman, younger than he by about fifteen years at least, would never ever show any interest in him at all, but still, she was on his mind just about all the time. His last thoughts at night before going to sleep, were of her, and the first thing when he arose. Maybe, he should just come out and tell her, and if she laughed in his face, then so be it. He was a big boy and he would soon get over her!

That was what he would do. He would tell her on their next date, and he would be crossing all of his fingers and toes!

At 4:30, he told Rosie, who was on duty by this time, where he was going and who he was going to meet. He told her that if he didn't check in with her by 6:00 P.M., to send the crew on duty to rescue him.

"Chief," she answered, a little fear in her voice,"do you think that's such a good idea. I mean, it's just like the rabbit walking into the fox's mouth!"

Bill liked her way of putting it, but he told her, "Do not say anything to anyone at all unless I don't check in, okay?"

"I understand, Chief, I understand, but I don't like it, no not at all!"

He parked in front of the restaurant at 4:59 and walked to the front door, and just as he reached it, the door swung open, and Larry stood there.

He didn't say a word, but motioned for Bill to come on in, which Bill did, but did not turn his back to Larry.

Larry motioned for Bill to follow him to a table in the back, and they set down. Larry had a fresh pot of coffee made and he offered Bill a cup, but Bill refused, saying, "I don't drink coffee."

He looked Larry straight in the eyes and asked, "What do you want to talk about?"

Larry took a sip of the hot brew, sat his cup down, and said, "I just wonder why you have included me in this secret investigation you're conducting."

"What makes you think I am including you in this investigation, anyway," asked Bill.

"Because you were looking at my pickup, and you said as much when I questioned you," said Larry vehemently.

"For your information, Larry, everyone in this town is considered a suspect, until the case is completed," said Bill, trying to keep a civil voice.

"What is this case," Larry asked again.

"I told you once before, I am not at liberty to say, so don't ask me again," he said very sternly.

"Okay, okay, don't get your panties in a wad, I was just curious," he answered.

"But," Bill asked, "you can tell me what you were doing up on the old Rogers Plantation the other day."

Larry squirmed a little, and asked, "How do you know I was up there and what if I was?"

"I know you were up there because I matched your tire treads against the tracks that were there, and the mud on your truck matches the type of mud that's up there," he said.

"So what if I did go up there, is that a crime," Larry asked.

"It is when there is yellow-police crime 'do not-molest' tape that's up, and you decide to cross it or better yet, deliberately tear it down, then it becomes a crime, maybe a small crime, but still a crime nonetheless," said Bill.

Larry laughed and said, "You'd actually put me in jail for that?"

Bill didn't laugh, but answered, "As Gabby Hayes used to say, 'you're dern tootin' I would, and I ought to!"

Larry said in a sarcastic way, "Chief, if I was you, I'd think twice about putting me in jail."

Bill looked at him, and asked, "Just why should I think twice about putting you in jail?"

Larry, laughed sarcastically again, and said, "We both happen to know a beautiful young blond headed woman that works here and I believe that you really care about, if you catch my drift."

Bill jumped to his feet real fast and grabbed Larry by the collar of his shirt and yanked him up out of his chair, causing the table to fall at the same time. The move was so fast that it surprised Larry, and he was caught completely off guard.

Bill was very angry, and Larry could see this, and now wished he had kept his mouth shut.

Bill, shoved him against the wall, and got right up in his face, and said very angrily, "I want to make something very, very clear. If anything, and I do mean anything, such as a fall or a broken fingernail, I'm coming to see you. I'm coming with my badge off, and I'm going to make you feel so bad, that you will wish you had never seen me or Mary Jo. So you see, you'd better, for your own sake, keep her from all harm, at all times, because, buster, I am not kidding in the least!"

Larry never knew that one man could have that much reaction in him, in fact Larry wasn't one to scare easily, but he was afraid of this man. He made a mental note to make sure that he watched over Mary Jo, because he felt as if, Bill would like nothing better, than find an excuse to work him over, or better yet, take him out.

"Sure, Chief, sure," he kept repeating, "I truly like Mary Jo myself, and I wouldn't allow anything to happen to her, even if I could. Don't you know that?" He was beginning to whine.

"Well, you heard me, and I meant what I said, "Bill said again, angrily.

"Sure, Chief, sure, I understand," he spoke softly, as Bill walked out of the restaurant.

Bill quickly stuck his head back in the door and said forcefully, "Don't tell Mary Jo about this. If she finds out, then I'll know it came from you and I'll be mighty unhappy. Things will go along between me and you as nothing had happened. Understand?"

Larry raised his hand, giving Bill the high sign and said, "She'll never learn from me, and nothing has happened between you and I!"

Bill waved back and was gone.

It took Larry awhile to stop trembling, and then he cleaned up the spilled coffee, and realized that in all his life, even during his tour in the Marine Corps, and in Iraq, he had never been scared of a single person. But, this man had scared the living daylights out of him, so he checked his pants to see if they were still dry, and he felt between the legs, and they were.

Bill drove around in his patrol car, giving himself enough time to get over his mad spell, as he didn't want to pick-up Mary Jo, with a scowl on his face, and a bad thought on his mind. He had good news to tell her. The City Council had approved hiring a new patrolmen/woman, and he was going to give the job to her, if she still wanted it.

CHAPTER 13

Bill and Mary Jo had gone to Clinton to the Steakhouse, and enjoyed a great meal, and after eating, they had rode down to the park, that was built around a large lake, near the center of town. They picked a bench, under some oak trees, and sat down. They watched as the sun finally went down below the horizon, and there was not much talk between them.

Finally Mary Jo asked, "Why did you ask me if I had told anyone about you going to the Sheriff's office. Was it supposed to be a secret?"

"No, not really," he answered, "but, I only told two people, you and one other."

"But, I still don't understand why it's so important," she questioned.

"Well, if you must know, I was ambushed on the way to Clinton yesterday morning. They missed me, but blew out the back window on my patrol car!"

"Oh, my goodness," she said excitedly, "why didn't you tell me. Who would do such a thing?"

He explained the case of the disappearances of the people from Rogersville, and his greatest desire to solve it. He believes that it all started here in Rogersville, and he must find out why, and where and what. All of those people were some of his best friends, and he wanted them back.

"Do you believe that Larry is the one that shot at you," she asked.

"I can't prove it, but I strongly suspect it, I really do," he said.

She sat back, and he said he was depending on her to keep all this to herself.

263

"Oh, I will, I will, in fact, if there's any way I can help, I want to," she said excitedly.

"After telling you this, I have a question, do you still want to be a policewoman on our police force?" he asked.

She looked at him with a question in her eyes, and said, "oh, yes, more now than ever!"

"Do you believe you can take orders from me?" he asked

"If I can't take orders from you, then I can't take orders from anyone," she answered.

He didn't say anything else, and she was waiting, but he just sat back, without another word, and this made her want to bop him one, because she was certain he was going to tell her about the open patrolmen's position, but he stopped short.

She stood it as long as she could, and poked him in the ribs, and asked, "Well, are you going to tell me or not?"

"Tell you what," he asked.

"You know, about the patrolman's job!"

"Oh that, it is yours, if you still want it," he said in a lackadaisically way, knowing it was aggravating her.

"You know I still want it," she said excitedly, "when do I start?"

"We have to do the usual background check, and," he stopped and looked straight in the eyes, "you are not wanted by the F.B.I. or anyone are you?"

She poked him in the ribs again, and said, "You better hope and pray I'm not, because look how bad it would be for you because you have been running around with me!"

He laughed and said, "Well, my defense would be that I knew you were a dangerous person, and I was keeping you close, so that I could get the goods on you before making the final arrest!"

"Oh, and you would too," she laughed.

Bill told her he had an idea and he asked her, "Can you get out of the restaurant at exactly 2:00 tomorrow, and if you can, I'll let you help me on a project."

"Just be there waiting on me with the motor running, and I'll be out that front door at exactly, 2:00P.M!"

Mary Jo felt as if Bill had something else to say to her and she waited, but he dragged around on a few unimportant things, so she figured the ball was in her court, and she put his face between her soft hands and said, "You know, Bill Freeway, I Love You!" Bill sit there as if he was frozen, then a big smile crossed his face and he kissed her as sweetly as he knew, and he said, "I have been trying to get up the courage to tell you how I feel, but I was so afraid that you weren't interested in an old man like me!"

She smiled and hugged him real tight and said, "I think I fell in love with you the morning that Rosie had fell. You showed so much compassion for one of your employees, and you don't see much of that!"

He was sitting out front at exactly 2:00 P.M., and sure enough, she came bounding out the door, smiling, and jumped into the front seat, touched him on the arm, and said, "Hello, you big hunk of a man!"

Bill returned the favor, and said, "Hello yourself, you very, beautiful hunk of woman!"

With that, she suddenly reached over and kissed Bill to his surprise. Then she buckled up and said, "Let's go, I'm ready, if you are."

He explained to Mary Jo, that he didn't know what he was really looking for. He had been told that it might be a good place to start in the disappearance of the citizens of Rogersville."

"So, you think it may be property or something of that nature that has a connection to the mystery." she asked.

They pulled into the courthouse, and immediately went to the room that had all the maps of the county, and the current and past landowners. Both Bill and Mary Jo started searching through the very large books, when all of a sudden, Bill let out a soft yell,   "Mary Jo, look what I've found. Come see."

Mary came over and said, "What is that except a colored map?"

"This is a plat showing a portion of the old Rogers Plantation, and if you'll notice it is divided into 4-fourty acre sections."

"Okay, I see that, so what now," she asked.

"Now, look here and you'll see who owns these sections," he pointed to a page attached to the plat.

"Wow," she said," now I'm beginning to see what this is all about, land, and somebody wants it."

"Correct, but why do they want it, is our next question," he shook his head slightly.

"Chief, I do believe that you can, with all your wisdom, figure this out," she said.

"Well, figure it out, I will, I certainly will," he said as they walked out of the courthouse.

The next day, being Friday, Mary Jo was off for the weekend, so Bill came up with the idea, for Mary Jo and him to go camping on the 160 acres of land that was under question. Maybe, they could mix business with pleasure, and scout around for clues, and at the same time, enjoy the pleasure of each other's company.

At 2:00 P.M., he was waiting outside the restaurant for Mary Jo, to emerge from her work, and about 2:25, she walked out, and was surprised to see him sitting there. She came to the truck, and asked what he was doing.

He asked her if she enjoyed camping, and she said, "It's according who with!"

He stared at her with an exasperated look, but said nothing. She stood there for a moment, then, shook him, and said, "What's the matter, cat got you tongue?"

"No," he replied, "but a certain lass named Mary Jo Knowles, just took my breath away. She has caused a great pain to pass through my heart as if a lightning bolt had struck, but other than that, I'm okay!"

Mary Jo laughed, and struck him on the arm, "You know, I could really get to, well, get real close to a big, handsome fellow like you, especially on a camping trip!"

He smiled, and said, "Well, hop in my lady, I've got everything we need to go camping, except, we've need to go by and pick up some clothes for you."

When they arrived at the road leading to the property, they discovered that they gate was locked, blocking the road.

Bill got out, rambled through his tool box, and pulled out a pair of metal clippers, and proceeded

272

to cut the lock. He then swung the gate open, and she drove the truck through.

He reached into his pocket, and pulled out a roll of yellow 'Police Line-Do Not Cross' tape and stretched it across the opening after shutting the gate.

They slowly drove up the road, searching for a suitable camping site, and at the same time, looking all around. They finally found a nice spot on some soft green grass, near a small creek, and under some spreading oak trees.

Bill, soon had the tent up, and a fire going, and Mary Jo, was working on fixing something for supper. Soon, she had selected something, and the smell of the steaks cooking on an open fire was driving Bill crazy, as he didn't believe they would ever get ready.

After they had eaten, they were lying around, as the sky turned dark, and the stars came out, Bill told her he was certainly glad she had come with him.

She turned towards him and said, "Don't you know by now, that I truly enjoy your company. Can't you see it in my eyes?"

He leaned forward, and made the comic look of peering in her eyes, and she playfully slapped him, and he wrestled her down, and started tickling her.

"Oh, no, please don't do that! I can't stand that," she begged.

He stopped and brought her up and gave her a long kiss, and when he stopped for breath, she went limp in his arms.

In a moment, she gradually sat up, and he looked at her, straight in her eyes, and said truthfully, "I did not bring you with me, for a one-night stand, do you understand. I think way too much of you, do you understand?"

She took Bill's head in her hands, and said, slowly, "If I had thought that you did, I would not have come. I am not a one-night stand for anybody. I think too much of you too, Bill Freeway, to allow such a thing. Now, do you understand?"

The next morning, while Mary Jo was preparing breakfast, Bill walked around the campsite, and when he got to the truck, he stopped, and looked down. There were boot prints all around the back of the truck.

He quickly made an inventory, but did not notice anything was missing. He decided not to tell Mary Jo, as he didn't want to frighten her.

Later on, they walked up to a little rise that had a water seepage coming out of the side that flowed down and into the small creek. Bill examined the water, and the ground around it, but found nothing unusual.

They walked back to the campsite, and had sandwiches and chips for lunch, and while they were eating, Bill asked, "Mary Jo, can you shoot a pistol?"

She looked at him with a quizzical look, and said, "Yes, yes, I can, as a matter of fact, my Dad taught me how."

"That's good," he said, and he walked to the pickup, and brought out two pistols, a .38 snub-nose, and a 9 millimeter automatic. He walked over to Mary Jo, and handed her the .38, and said, "Here, keep this handy. I have a feeling we're being watched."

"Oh, my goodness," she said, "do you really think that someone is watching us?"

He told her about the foot prints around the truck, and his feelings of someone or others watching every move they make! He also told her of his rifle, a .343 rifle and cartridges behind the seat of the truck, in case it's needed.

They searched some more in the afternoon, but found nothing of note, they, in the morning, loaded up their camping equipment, and moved further onto the land.

They passed a small clump of trees sitting on top of a small hill off to their left, and the road was getting really rough, so he slowed down considerably, almost to a crawl.

They had gone about a few hundred feet from the clump of trees, when they saw, what looked as if someone had been digging at a spot upon the side of this small mound.

Bill put the truck in 4-wheel drive and up to the top of the mound they went. When he got there, he discovered that digging had indeed been taking place. Both he and Mary Jo had jumped out, and Bill also grabbed a shovel off the back.

He walked around, but could not see anything out of the ordinary about the spot. He dug up a few shovelfuls of dirt, but nothing unusual.

They walked up into the small clump of vines, bushes and saplings, at the top of the mound. Bill said, "I think I have hit zero again, my lady."

But before Mary Jo could answer, the whine of a bullet went through the air, just above their heads.

Bill instinctively grabbed Mary Jo, and shoved her down on the ground, and said, "Stay put!"

As he said that, another bullet whined through the bushes, and the sound of a high-powered rifle was heard. Then another, but this time, the bullet must have hit low, in the dirt, near the truck.

He crawled over to where he could slightly see over the lip of the mound, and he saw what he thought was two rifles, pointing at them, from the clump of trees he had spotted across the road.

He fired his 9 millimeter, but he knew they were too far away to do any good, but it made them duck for a moment, but surely, they would catch on pretty soon!

He had to get to his rifle in the truck, but how? It was wide open from the bushes to the truck. He would be an easy target. But, he would have to try it. He had an idea.

He asked Mary Jo to crawl up there, to keep her head down, and she did. He handed her his 9 millimeter, and told her what to do. He crawled down to the edge of the bushes, and turned to Mary Jo, and signaled. She stuck the gun up over the edge, and started firing the pistol.

He jumped up, and remembering his Army Ranger training, he dashed, back and forth until he reached his truck. They had spotted him and took several shots, but all they did was make spouts of dirt at his feet,

He eased open the door, trying real hard to not show any of his head, he reached behind the seat, and withdrew the rifle. He jacked in a shell, and putting a box of cartridges in his pocket, he started back to Mary Jo.

When he got to the back of the truck, he quickly, raised the rifle, and shot towards the trees where the two men were standing. It must have hit close, so they jumped back into the dark of the trees.

Bill broke running hard and dove into the spot where Mary Jo was lying. She was very glad to see him.

"Well, big boy, I see you made it after all. Is there any holes in you?"

"You didn't hear me yell out now, did you," he relied.

"You were running so hard, I didn't think you had time to yell out," she laughed.

"Funny, funny," he said sarcastically, "I see you need a lesson in respecting your betters!"

"When I meet one, then I'll be glad to take lessons," she guffawed.

Bill put his finger to his closed lips to quiet her, and they listened for a few minutes, and no sound came except an occasional wisp of wind, and a bird singing. He slowly, raised his head, and looked over the lip, and stared, and told her to stay here again.

He moved out of the cover easily, and kept a sharp eye on the place where the shooting was coming from.

He moved to stand beside the truck, and watched for about one-half hour, and was completely satisfied, that no one was still there.

He told Mary Jo to come on out, and when she got to the truck, he asked her how good was she with a rifle, and she answered, her Dad took her deer hunting all the time.

283

"Good," he said, and he handed her the rifle and pointed to the spot where the shooting had been coming from, "keep this scope on that place, and if there is any movement over there, shoot right above their heads."

"Above their heads," she sounded disappointed, "why not between their eyes?"

"Wow," he retorted, "you are a bloodthirsty dame aren't you?"

"Nope, I just don't like scum hiding out and taking pot shots at me and my lover, that's all!"

He hesitated for a moment at what she said, then inserted a new clip in the 9 millimeter and went around the truck and started running towards the spot he had showed her. He was expecting a shell to hit him at any time, but none came, and when he came to a large stump, he dove behind it.

He lay still for a moment to catch his breath and looked back at Mary Jo, and she gave him the high sign, and he jumped up and continued his run towards the sniper's spot.

When he got there, he slipped the safety off, to fire, and was ready to exchange shots with anyone there, but they were gone. Nothing left but two sets of boot prints, some empty rifle cartridges, .30-.06 caliber and .243. He picked these up and put them in his pocket, and he also found a wrapper for a 'El Rialto" cigar. He knew that this was a good clue, because not too many men, if any, around Rogersville, smoked this brand, simply because they were too expensive.

In a few minutes, Mary Jo walked up, her rifle at the ready, and said, almost shouting, "You dummy, I thought something had happened to you. You came in here but you didn't come out!"

He took her in his arms and held her, and she was actually trembling, so he just held her until she settled down, and then turned her face towards his, and planted a long, sweet kiss upon her lips.

She sighed, and said, "Oh, Bill, I was so worried. I suppose you know by now, that I care a lot about you, big, old dummy!"

He laughed, and asked, "How can you care about me and call me a dummy?"

She laughed, and answered, "My Mom and Dad always told me to take care of the half-witted people I come across, and I guess you fill that bill."

"Well, I guess I do fit that bill," he said softly, "I'd be more than happy for you to take care of me for the rest of my life."

"They don't call me Nurse Mary Jo for nothing," she said.

Bill said, I'd really like to stand all day here with you, but I need to follow those boot prints, and see where they lead to."

"Lead on, Daniel Boone, Davy Crockett, is right behind you!"

They followed the boot prints through the thick woods, across a wet weather stream, and soon they came to a clearing. Bill stopped there without exposing themselves, and they could see an old ramshackle house, across a county road.

Someone was home, because, there was smoke coming from the chimney. Bill could see the prints, and they led to an old barb-wire fence, straight across from the house.

They stood in the woods for about an hour, but could see no one. There was a thunderstorm building up, so he and Mary Jo hurried back through the woods, and just as they reached the pickup, it came a downpour. Bill,once was afraid that they wouldn't make it out, but the four-wheel drive, took hold, and they made it back to the county road and home.

He was anxious to visit the old ramshackle house, but he would not put Mary Jo's life in danger again. Two days was enough, and he hoped that, that would never happen again.

When he got to where she lived, he told her he was sorry about what went on, and sh surprised him by saying, "Don't be sorry. Man, that's the most fun I've had in a long, long time. I could do that every weekend. Makes your blood boil, you know?"

Bill looked surprised, and couldn't speak, so she said, "What, have I surprised the big, tough Chief? Well, don't be. I was brought up in a house of brothers, who, in one way or another, were law-dogs, or military, so you see, it's not new to me."

He looked at her with a question, and she asked, "Come on and ask me, I know you have a question?"

"Yes, I do, but it will wait until tomorrow night," he said.

"Oh, can't meet you tomorrow night," she replied quickly, as she got out of the truck, "I've got another date."

Before he could say anything, she was already in the house and all he could do was head for home, thinking, "I thought that we had something going. In fact, I was so sure of it, I was thinking seriously of asking her to marry me, but, it's lucky you didn't make a fool out of yourself."

CHAPTER 14

He went to the restaurant and had breakfast, and Mary Jo was smiling at him, but he decided that the best thing to do was to just, be friendly, and forget all about her as his bride.

After he had eaten, he invited Larry to sit down, and surprisingly, Larry did. Bill asked him if he was a hunting man, and if so, what did he hunt for.

Larry really opened up, and said he liked to hunt whitetail deer. He had done a lot of that in his home state of Virginia, going out with the fellows on a cold, snowy morning.

Bill laughed slightly, and said, "Don't expect too many snowy mornings around here, cold, yes but, not much snow."

"I know. I've learned that from talking to some of the guys that come in here," answered Larry.

"Say, "said Bill, "my favorite is a .243 caliber, or an 8 millimeter magnum. I find that they are the best around here. What do you use?"

"I like the lever action, .30-06," Larry replied, "I found that I can hit most what I shoot at."

Bill wanted to jump up and shout, but held his peace. Now he knew where the .30-.06, now if he would just light up a cigar, but he didn't, and Bill told him they would have to do some hunting when the season came in this fall.

Bill walked out after paying his bill without speaking to Mary Jo and all she could do was watch him go, wondering what the problem was with him.

Bill, after checking in at headquarters decided to make a trip up to the old house. He wanted to see, just what he could see. If someone lived there, then all the better, he could question them, and maybe find the answer to some questions.

When he arrived at the driveway, he slowly drove in towards the old house. There was smoke, coming from the chimney again, so someone was at home or nearby.

He made sure that his pistol was loaded, and as he got out of the patrol car, he stuck in the holster. He looked around, and slowly, carefully, approached the front of the house. The porch overhang looked as if it was about to fall at any minute, so he decided to knock on the side of the house, but no one answered. He knocked again, still no answer.

He eased around the corner of the house, and he saw an elderly black man, apparently feeding hogs in a pen, about, 50 feet behind the house.

Bill yelled, "Hello!"

The black man jumped, almost spilling his feed, and turned and seeing Bill said, "Whoa, mister, you scared the living daylights outta me!"

Bill said, apologetically, "I didn't mean to do that, but I need to talk to you. It's important."

When he said that, he thought he heard movement in the house, but the wind was blowing, so it might been the old house moving. Anyway, he was going to be on guard.

The black man came walking back to the house and asked, "You said you wanted to talk to me?"

"Yes, I do, what is your name," Bill asked.

"My name is Roscoe Battles," he said proudly.

"I am Bill Freeway, Chief of Police of Rogersville, Do you know anything about that property over there across the road?" Bill pointed to the land across the road from the old house.

"Yes sir, I does, I takes care of that property ever since Mr. Rogers grandpa was alive," he said proudly.

"Where is the old home spot," Bill asked.

"You have to get on dat road over dere and just keep going until you runs into it. The old plantation home is gone, but there is a few of the brick pillars still there and a birdbath and a few other things!"

"Have you seen anyone fooling around over there, anyone at all," Bill asked.

"No sir, I has the only key to the gate that I knows of, and I don't let anyone in, no sir, no one," he said.

"I had to break the lock, and apply police tape, because I believe that it part of a case I am working on," Bill said.

"Yes sir," said Roscoe.

"So, I'd appreciate it if you would leave the tape up for the time being," he said.

"Yes sir, I certainly will, you can count on that," answered Roscoe.

"You're certain that there has been no one that you know of fooling around on that property at all," Bill asked one more time before leaving.

Roscoe looked down at his feet and shuffled around some, then without looking up, said, "No sir, I ain't seen no one over there!"

Bill felt he was lying, but what could he do, threaten to shoot him?

He turned, and walked back to his car, and had the feeling that another pair of eyes was watching him beside Roscoe's, but he didn't see anyone. So, he drove down the road and pulled into the road that led to the plantation. He sat there for a few minutes, and he decided to go back and see if Roscoe would accompany him to the old plantation site.

He backed out and drove to Roscoe's and as he was pulling up in the drive, he could have sworn he heard a shot, possibly a small caliber, such as a .22.

He rushed up to the old house, and pulling his pistol, heard footsteps running out the backdoor, and he ran to the corner, and eased his head around it. But no one was in sight.

He noticed the back door was wide open, so he rushed into it, and there was Roscoe, apparently, fixing to eat a meal. Bill, when he got closer, knew that Roscoe was dead and he examined him, he saw that someone had shot him in the back of the head and he had fallen forward.

Bill knew also, that the shooter was still around, because the smell of gunpowder was still strong in the room, and he had heard the killer run out.

He used his mike, called Jimmy, told him the situation, and told him to contact the Sheriff, since this was out of the Police Jurisdiction, and that he believed he was after the killer.

"10-4, Chief, and you be careful. I'm contacting Jack and Buford and getting them up there to assist you," said Jimmy, the dispatcher.

"Thanks, Jimmy," was all Bill could say, as he walked to the back door and surveyed the area. There were only three buildings, a barn, a pig sty, and an outhouse. He couldn't be in the barn, because it was in plain view as he drove in, so it only left the pig sty, and the outhouse.

He said, "Eeny-meeny-mineey-mo, to the pig-sty, I go," and he took off running to the pig sty, and as he ran around it, it was obvious, no one was there.

So, that left the outhouse, and you got to admire him for staying in there during all this terrible heat and that terrible smell, but it's up to me to get him out.

Bill took a deep breath and with his pistol at the ready, rushed to the side of the outhouse, and he thanked someone, because they had built so well, that there was no cracks in the side.

When he got in position, he was just fixing to yell, when the door opened, flung back, and Bill heard someone running away. He eased around the corner, and took aim at the fleeing man, and yelled, "Halt, Police!"

The man turned, and fired at Bill, and hit him in the left shoulder, and Bill instinctively, pulled the trigger, and the man screamed, through up his arms and hit the ground.

Bill cautiously approached the groaning figure on the ground, and seeing the pistol he had dropped, he kicked it away. He knelt down and his bullet had hit the man just below his neck and it was certain he was dying.

He looked up at Bill and said, "Man, that was a lucky shot you made, hitting me, you know."

"Hang on, "Bill said, "I'll get a doctor up here."

"No need to," the man coughed, "I'm done for."

"Have you got anyone that I need to contact," asked Bill.

"No, I am an orphan," he coughed again, this time harder, and spitting up blood, "there's no one to cry over me, but probably a lot that'll be glad I'm gone."

"Who did you work for," asked Bill.

But his question went unanswered, as the killer was staring into space, but not seeing anything.

The Sheriff soon arrived, and there was a hearing was held several days later, and it was determined that Bill fired in self-defense, and the killers gun was a .22 caliber, and his fingerprints were the only ones on it. Also, Roscoe's wound was caused by a .22 caliber, the weapon used by most hit men.

Bill was sitting at home watching the Braves play when the telephone rang. He answered, and what was usually a very soft voice, was tense, and very upset as she said, "Bill, why haven't you called me. I was very hurt when I found out you were shot, and you didn't call me. I cried and cried, right there in the restaurant. Marjorie had a very tough time getting me to stop!"

Bill who was glad to finally get in a word, said, "I didn't think you cared anymore, besides it was only a flesh wound."

"I'm coming out there right now. I'll be there in a few minutes," she said, loudly, and slammed the phone down before he could say another word.

CHAPTER 15

True to her word, within a short time, Bill saw her headlights through the front windows, and in a few moments, there was a loud knocking on his front door. "Bill, open this door, I know you're in there," came her voice.

Bill rushed to the door. Afraid she just might break it down, and opened I, and she rushed past him, and set herself down on the couch, said, "Now, what's this about I don't care for you anymore?"

He walked to the couch, and motioned for her to slide over a little, said as he was sitting down, said, "Just what I said, if you remember, when I took you home, after the camping trip, I asked if you wanted to go somewhere for supper the next night and you said no, you had a date. So, I decided that you had found someone else."

"Why, you big, dumb-ox," she said, "yes, I had another date, but not with another man. I had to take my landlady to a church social that I had promised her I would about a month ago. Don't you remember me telling you?"

Bill felt very foolish, and then he remembered that indeed, she had mentioned it to him. He had had so much on his mind lately, that it was a wonder that he even remembered his own name.

He dropped his head, took her hands, and said softly, "Do you forgive me. I truly forgot that you said that. I've been running in circles so much lately, but I try not to forget anything between you and I. That's way too important!"

"I forgive you." She leaned over and lightly kissed him on the lips, and he was grateful that she did.

She said, "I need to see where my big-boy was wounded, she said, "Take your shirt off."

He started to protest, but the look on her face told him that it was no use, so he pulled the tee over his head and she examined the wound, after carefully removing the bandage,

She sat there looking at it, and then started sobbing softly, and said, "Just a few inches further to the left, and you wouldn't be here, you know that?"

He felt real bad now that he had ever not believed her. He now felt she had a strong attraction for him, and this made him feel a whole lot better, as he knew he had a very strong attraction for her. In fact, it was so strong for her, that he desired to make her his bride, but he was afraid to ask right now.

She replaced the bandage with some fresh bandages, that Bill had, and they popped some popcorn, and watched the remainder of the ballgame, which the Braves won handily.

When the ball game was over, she stood up and was preparing to leave, but Bill wished her to stay a little longer. She said, she would like to, but 4:00 A.M. came awful early, and she had to get back to her room, and take a shower, and get to bed.

Bill relented, but he made her promise to call him as quick as she walked into her room, so he would know if she made it all right. She agreed to, and gave him a sweet, strong, long, good night kiss, and he nearly fell, it made him so dizzy.

Sure enough, when she arrived, she called as promised, and just as she was hanging up, she said, "I love you, big man."

Bill said, "I love you too," but she had already hung up. He debated whether to call her or not, but decided to let her shower and get her sleep.

He did call headquarters, and asked Rosie, "Did you know Roscoe Battles?"

Rosie said, "Not personally, Chief. I've seen him at church on Sunday when ever I've had the occasion to go, but of course, I have to work every other weekend."

"Is there any other thing that you might have heard about him," asked the Chief.

"I've heard some of the sisters and my mom speak once in a while, and especially since he has been killed, that he has a daughter down in Mobile, that's got a bad disease, cancer, I think, and she's in and out of the hospital all the time, and he's been sending every cent he could rake and scrape to her and her kids!"

"That explains his part in this mystery, and what does he have to show for it. Not a dad-blame thing. That's what. Now he's dead, and she has no money coming in at all,"

he said, very vehemently.

He decided to ask Mary Jo to go with him up to the courthouse once more, as he just had an idea. He wanted to check on some more things and see if history had a part in all this.

At 2:00 P.M., he picked up Mary Jo, and they headed to the courthouse in Clinton. He knew they would have to hurry, because, it closed at 4:00 P.M.

He went into the clerk's office and asked the lady, if she had a book of old newspapers, from say over 100 years ago. She said, "of course", but they would have to sign in and out. They did so, and Bill came up with a question.

He asked the lady if he could have a copy of the sign in sheet for the last two months. She said she could only do it for duly appointed officers of the court or of the law. He showed her his badge and identification, and she immediately walked to the back and started making copies.

Bill and Mary Jo walked into the room, and looked up and down the rows of old ledgers, and finally, decided to start around, 1850, and read all the newspapers pertaining to this area.

They did so, and around 3:30, Mary Jo, came across an article, in the June 1865 copy of the Clinton Free Press. She called it to Bill's attention, and he and she started reading the well, worn article.

The article "stated that a steamboat had been robbed in broad daylight, of $2,500.000 and the robbers had gotten away. No arrests had been made. The $2,500,000 was".... And the newspaper was torn, and the rest of the article was missing.

"Wow," Bill said, "do you have any idea what $2,500,000 is worth in today's currency, especially if it's gold!"

"More than we can count," she said breathlessly.

"Chief, it's time we are closing," came the tiny voice from the other room.

"Coming," he said, as they walked towards the other room. The tiny lady had his sign in sheets ready for him, and he thanked her on the way out.

On the way back to Rogersville, they discussed the stolen gold, or whatever, and Bill fixed it in his mind, that was what all this was about.

He asked Mary Jo, if she in for another camping trip and she eagerly answered yes, if it's with you, I certainly am. They both laughed.

Saturday morning, Bill pulled up in front, and Mary Jo came out carrying a small bag, and a cooler. Bill got out of the truck, and helped her put it in the back.

She jumped in the seat and scooted over close to him and said, "Good morning, my tall-man." And she reached around and kissed him full on the lips.

This maneuver surprised him, but it was very delightful, and he almost decided not to move the truck, but to just sit there and neck, like a couple of teenagers!

But at her urging, he put it in gear and started up to the property, and soon was arriving at the old plantation sit. They knew they were there, because the horseshoe drive was still well outlined, a few brick pillars were still standing, several rose bushes were in plain sight, some with multi-colored flowers.

They got out, and the first thing Bill noticed was a birdbath, right in the middle of the drive, with a small metallic cupid, with his bow drawn back and a arrow, ready to launch. The tub was full of trash, so Bill cleaned it out, so other birds could wash and drink.

He and Mary Jo walked over to old site where the home stood, and stood in the middle, and Mary Jo said, "Listen Bill, can't you hear the fiddles,

314

and violins, and the pianos, and the singing, at a cotillion or a dance. See the ladies in their big long dresses, and the men in their coats, and string ties, can't you just see it?"

"Yes, "he said, "but what I can't see or hear is the hum of the air conditioners, or the televisions, and the Atlanta Braves playing."

"Oh, you," she said, and pushed him, "you don't have any history in you at all, do you?"

"On the contrary," he laughed, "right now I am full of it. I think that $2,500,000 is buried right here, somewhere on this old plantation site."

When they had finished eating supper, and Bill had helped Mary Jo in cleaning up the dishes, pots and pans, he took out a map of the old Rogers Plantation.

When he showed it to Mary Jo, she remarked about the different colors, and he said that he had took some color magic markers, and colored, the different plots. In the very middle, right where they pitched their tent and made camp, was the Plantation home site, and it actually sat in the corner of all four –forty acre sections, owned by the missing families.

Bill really felt that this was the place to start. He knew if the money was found, it would go to the owner of the section, it was found on. Someone was going to be filthy rich. Hopefully, they were still alive to be able to enjoy their new found riches. Hopefully, he prayed!

They looked over the map, carefully, and then looked again, hoping that they had missed something, but sadly they hadn't. He got up, walked to the birdbath, and laid the map on top, and again tried to discover something that maybe he and Mary Jo had overlooked.

He turned the map so that the north arrow was pointing north, compared the area as best he could in the failing light, and was fixing to roll up his map, when it caught his eye.

He bent down, and sighted along the arrow of cupid, standing tall in the birdbath. "Mary Jo, come here please," he called out.

In a few minutes she was there, and asked what did he want? He said, "Bend down and look straight down the arrow of our little friend, Mr. Cupid!"

She did as he asked, and said, "I see a tree, and this 'arrow' almost splits it in half. It is showing a straight line to it."

"That's what I think also," he said, "maybe it's our first clue, but we'll have to wait until tomorrow to see for sure."

When morning came, Bill was at the birdbath while Mary Jo was preparing breakfast, the bacon she was cooking, sure did smell mighty good,

He saw the tree that Mary Jo had told him about last night, and he could see, other trees, in a straight line, behind the first one.

He got Mary Jo to guide him as he walked towards the tree. She would yell, "go right" or "go left", and as he was walking along, he stubbed his toe on something that was barely sticking out of the ground. He bent down, and taking his shovel, he dug around it, and seceded it was what was left of a large post, probably, a corner post, of the stables, that used to be here. He dragged his boot towards what, in his mind, might be the other corner, and he dug around some, but no luck.

He yelled back to Mary Jo, and was back on his way towards the tree. Soon, he was at the outer limbs of the oak tree, whose limbs, were all the way to the ground. He walked all around it searching for a clue, or anything that might prove he was on the right trail, but so far, nothing!

Mary Jo soon joined him, and she had brought a hatchet, and a bush axe. She had seen the low hanging limbs.

Bill took the bush-axe, and started on the south side, and all Mary Jo could do, was watch, as the hatchet was really too short to reach into the tree to cut limbs. So, as Bill cut, she would pull them out of the way, and then pile them up.

Shortly, Bill had cut enough away, so they started examining the trunk of the big oak, and Mary Jo, said, "Bill, look here, I think I may have found something!"

Bill looked at what she had found, and took his hand and slowly outlined the figures with his finger. Satisfied, that there was something there, he decided to go real slow and interpret by feel, what was carved into the tree.

"Mary Jo," he asked, "do you have some paper to write on?"

She fumbled around in her pockets and came out with a piece of paper, an order ticket, like she used at the restaurant. Bill threw her his ball point pen, and she sat down and began to wait.

Bill stuck his finger back in the carving, and slowly, traced the figures there. He did it several times as he was confused, but when he finally realized he was feeling the same thing each time, he called it out, "Mary Jo, it has an arrow, pointing to the right, and below it, is the figure 10," and feeling around the carving some more, finally decided that was all!

Mary Jo jumped up and came to the tree, and put her back against it, looking east. She said to Bill, "I don't see anything special out there, except some storm clouds building up!"

Bill looked and she was right, and they were soon to get a deluge of rain.

He told her to come on, and they headed back to the campsite, and storing everything that might be harmed by rain, they decided to ride this storm out in the truck.

Bill and Mary Jo got in just as a few large drops hit the windshield, the wind sped up, and then lightning, and thunder. Pretty soon, rain was coming down, hard, and they sat there watching it run off the windshield, and trying to decipher the carving.

"Mary Jo said, "Bill, it's got to be 10 feet to the east from the tree, don't you think?"

"I don't know," he answered, "but, I wish this rain would hurry up and stop so we can go and see. I'm getting anxious!"

As if by magic, the rain suddenly stopped, the sun started showing from behind some of the dark clouds, and the wind died down.

"Wow," cried Mary Jo," I didn't know you had a hot line straight to the MASTER."

"I don't," he said, "I don't, HE just felt sorry for me. He knows how much I want to solve this mystery!"

"Well, I know who to come to, when I need a prayer answered," she said.

He started the truck and said, "I know what you want to do, and that's get out of work, but it won't work, young lady, it won't work, you hear!"

She laughed, and started to say something, but Bill held up his hands, as if to silence her. She laughed, and slapped him on his arm.

When they had measured off ten feet, Bill started digging, and the ground was real compact on top and digging was difficult. He had to rest often, but soon he broke through. When he was about six feet down, he climbed out of the hole, he told Mary Jo, this wasn't the spot.

Bill said that the 10, may mean ten yards, so they pulled off thirty feet, and again Bill started to dig, and again, no luck.

Bill, by now was very tired, so they decided to retire back to the campsite, and Bill laid down, and was soon fast asleep. Mary Jo done the same thing, putting her arm around him, and they lay there until late afternoon, when Bill arose

suddenly, and seeing it was growing dark, he

woke Mary Jo, and they started back to town.

Today being Sunday, both of them had to

return to work tomorrow.

CHAPTER 16

Bill was now almost 100% that 10 feet and 30

feet was not the answer to the 10 that was carved

on the tree. But, certainly it was not ten miles, so

what was left? What did surveyors measure in

back in those days? He was sure it was feet and

inches, but he must check an old surveyors report

to see, but that would mean going all the way back

to Clinton. He looked in the telephone directory

for surveyors, and he found one, who lived just outside of Rogersville. He immediately called, and a woman's voice answered the phone, saying, "This is Barnett's Surveyors. Sorry, we can't come to the telephone right now, but leave your name and number, and a brief message, and we'll get back to you!." Bill did, so, for now, all he could do was sit and wait.

Bill was hoping that Mr. Barnett could set him straight on the techniques, and the type of measurement they used in the 1850-`1870's time period.

He didn't have to wait too long, for when the telephone rang, he answered, and was glad the man on the other end was Barnett.

Bill introduced himself, and then asked if he had any idea, what was the type of measurement they used during the period of say, 1850 -1870?"

Mr. Barnett answered, "Why they used feet and inches, such as we do today." Bill's jaw dropped, and he was greatly disappointed in the answer, and was just fixing to thank him and hang-up, when all of a sudden, he added, "now, some of the old time surveyor's would use rods, instead of feet, and let me tell you, that really causes some confusion today,"

Bill's demeanor changed in a second, and he said, "Thanks, so very, very much, Mr. Barnett. You may have just helped me solve a crime."

"Well, if I have, I want to say, I'm glad I did, and any time you need me, just call."

"I will, sir, I will," he said, "you can count on it."

Now, why didn't he think of that? Sometimes, they used rods, instead of feet. Now, what is the length of a rod in feet? He jumped up from his desk, found his trusty Webster's, and looked up "rod."

The dictionary defined the length of a rod, as 'a measure of 5-1/2 lineal yards.' He quickly multiplied 5-1/2 times 3 and he came up with the answer of 16-1/5 feet, then 10 times that = 161.5 feet. So, that had to be it. That was the only measurement that made any sense. If it was any longer, it would have been down the side of the sheer bank that was about a twenty to thirty foot drop, and that didn't make sense at all.

He was very anxious for morning to come, so he called Mary Jo, and told her that he thought he had it figured out. That the ten stood for rods, and it was about 165.5 feet from the tree. He was anxious for daylight to come so he could head up there to start digging.

"Bill Freeway," she yelled into the telephone, "you better not go up there without me. I want to go with you. Besides, there might be some else that might have figured it out by now."

"But, Mary Jo, I don't know if I can wait that long," he almost whimpered.

"I don't care if you can or not,' she almost yelled again, "you better wait on me. I'll be out the door at exactly 2:00 P.M."

"Okay, for you, I'll do it," he finally relented.

"I knew you would," she said, "and I love you for it."

Bill paused for a moment, and asked, "Is that for real, or is it just an everyday quote?"

"Well, what do you think it is," she asked.

"I know what I want it to be," he said.

"What is that, Mr. Freeway?"

"That you truly love me as I do you."

He heard her suck in her breath, and the first thing he thought of was, that he had really fouled up royally now. He was afraid that he had just succeeded in probably losing her forever.

He heard her crying softly, and he said, "Mary Jo, I didn't mean to upset you. I'm sorry."

"Why you big dummy," she said between small sobs, "I've been waiting for you to tell me that for a long, long time, but you never would. I felt like you cared for me, but you were too stubborn to say it, you know."

"Well, this big dummy, as you call me, does love you, with all his heart!"

At 2 P.M., and as usual, he was waiting outside the restaurant, and they headed to the old Plantation site,

They unloaded the tools, and pulled off the 165.5 feet from the oak tree, in a eastwardly direction.

Bill started with his round point shovel and this was a sandy spot and soon he was down about five feet. He asked Mary Jo, to look through the sand as he threw it upon the edge of the hole.

He threw an extra, large spade full of dirt up on the top, and in a moment, he heard Mary Jo, scream and he jumped out of the hole, to see what was wrong,

She was pointing down at an object on the ground. He thought it maybe a snake, so he pulled his pistol, ready to fire, and seen her, shaking her head, so he bent down and discovered a human skull!

He stood up and held her, and said it was all right, it was probably a hundred to two hundred years old.

Mary Jo said, "I don't care, it's still a dead man's skull. I touched it, and it scared me.!"

"They can't hurt you, but they can make you hurt yourself," he laughed.

"Oh you," she said, and beat on his chest, "I can't help it. I was scared!"

He immediately dialed his cell phone, and the gruff voice answered, and Bill said, "Guess what, we may have hit the jackpot. We have just uncovered a skull, and some bones, looking to be about 100 to 200 years old!"

"That's great. I'm going to send my number one team over there right now. Will you and Mary Jo wait there until they get there?" he asked

"Yes sir, you bet we will. What is the approximate time we can expect them," Bill asked?

"Oh, give them about three hours, and by the way, you'd better get your Sheriff and Coroner up there too," he added.

"Will do just as quick as I am through talking to you, he said, and then as an afterthought, asked, "how did you know that the young lady I have helping me is named Mary Jo?"

"Why, hasn't she told you, she's told you, she is my youngest daughter," he said happily.

"Your daughter," Bill spat out, "why you old walrus, you could have at least told me, you know!"

"Now, Bill, don't be mad," he said, "she was afraid that you might hire out of our friendship and not on her own merit."

About that time, Mary Jo, who had been standing quietly by Bill's side, and listening to the conversation about her, she suddenly took the telephone away from Bill and said, "Daddy, why did you spoil it. I haven't had the chance to tell him yet!"

Gruff voice said, "Honey, I'm sorry, but you told me you were going to tell him today and I just assumed you already had!"

"Well, I hadn't. Maybe I can make it right with him. He's a level headed man, you know."

Later on, Bill hadn't said much to Mary Jo, and after he had called the Sheriff and the coroner, he just went back to the truck and set and waited.

Mary Jo walked around trying to stay away from him while he was digesting the news he had just received about her. Finally, she walked over to the tuck and he looked up, and she said, "Bill, I don't blame you if you are mad at me, but I was going to tell you today, but we got so wrapped up in this, that I didn't have a chance."

"I'm not mad, I don't guess," he said slowly, "just shocked is all. It was quite a blow hearing it from one of my oldest and dearest friends."

"Do you think that makes me love you any less," she asked.

"I don't know, you'll have to answer that."

"No, emphatically, No!" she almost yelled.

"It doesn't mean I love you any less, either!" With that, he pulled her close, held her tight and kissed her deeper than at any time before.

When he finished the kiss, he had to hold her, as she would have certainly fell to the ground. he held her tightly, until she could stand on her on.

They heard vehicles coming up the old road leading to the Plantation site, and soon there were two vans, and a truck pulling a trailer with a backhoe on it. Behind them was the Sheriff's car.

Bill waved them all on up to where he and Mary Jo were waiting., and they came up and the first man to jump out, was middle aged, about 6' 2" tall and had blond hair. He recognized Mary Jo right off, and said, "Why, hello, Mary Jo, I didn't expect to meet you up here, of all places!"

"Lieutenant Marshall, it's so good to see you too," she replied, "this is Chief Bill Freeway of Rogersville."

Bill stuck out his hand, and the Lieutenant said, "Yes, Chief, I've heard of you, not only as Chief of Police, but also as a former A.B.I. agent, and the good work you done."

Bill blushed, and said, "I hope that all you heard was good things, but what we have here is a puzzle." He guided the Lieutenant towards the hole, and on the way, he said, "We have, I'm afraid, either a burial ground, or maybe just a single grave. I thought it was a good idea to get the A.B.I. in on this mystery since you have all the up to date scientific equipment, and my little force certainly does not."

"I'll be glad to do what I can, but have you gotten the Sheriff and the county Coroner in on this," he asked.

""No, not yet," Bill answered.

"Then I can't do a thing until they give the go ahead. My hands are tied," Marshall said.

"Then let's see what they have to say," said Bill, looking around for them, and saw that they were talking to Mary Jo.

He walked up to them and told them they needed to okay the A.B.I. operations, before they start.

The Sheriff looked at the Coroner, and then he said, "I don't see why they can't, do you Doctor?"

"No, I don't see any reason why they can't carry on with their operations," the Coroner said, "but, I would like to know what your conclusions are."

"No problem," answered the Lieutenant, "we always send copies of our work to the local Sheriff, and we can include you."

When they had placed the backhoe in place over the hole, and the operator began to dig. He carefully placed each bucketful, in a different spot, so that the other men could sift through the dirt, and remove any particles that might be in line with the investigation.

They found another skull, and several more bones, and a spinal column, that was in fairly good shape. The Lieutenant took them inside the van and started an intensive examination of all the bones, especially the skulls.

Bill stepped in, and asked, "have you made any headway so far?"

"Yes, I think so," said the Lieutenant, "these skulls are of the Negroid race, and I'm pretty sure that the bones are also. I am almost sure that the skulls have bullet holes in them!"

"Bullet holes," Bill exclaimed, "why would they have been shot, unless it was to keep a big secret around here."

"Maybe," said the Lieutenant, "it's the secret you are searching for, don't you think?"

"Well, I certainly hope so, and if it is, it just might help me to find out what happened to my friends," said Bill.

There was a knock on the van door, and a young man stuck his head through the door opening and said, "Lieutenant, the backhoe operator has run into something, and wants you to come see!"

The Lieutenant and Bill rushed out of the van, and when they got to the hole, the operator was down in it, hunched down. He looked up and said, "I've run into something that's awfully strange!"

"What is it," asked the Lieutenant.

"Apparently," the operator said, "it's a steel plate, and it seems to be thick enough to keep me from breaking through with my backhoe bucket!"

With that, Bill followed the Lieutenant into the hole, and they knelt down, and examined the steel plate that was under the sand. They both agreed that they should let the operator continue on and completely uncover the plate.

When they were out of the hole, the operator began to uncover the steel plate, and it was soon apparent it was larger than was first thought!

An hour went by and he was still uncovering, and he had already uncover two pieces, lying side by side, approximately, 8 feet wide and about 10 feet long.

Bill, with Mary Jo standing beside him, was waiting and watching, and Bill was wondering why was these plates of steel lying out here, about 4 feet under the soil, and side by side. Are they the cover of something, or what?

Soon, the operator yelled that he had finally reached the outer edge of the steel plates. The Lieutenant came out of the van, and Bill, and

Mary Jo and he got back into the hole to see if there was any clue to these plates.

It had already gotten dark, and they had brought large lights that were operated by a large generator, and they lit up the area as if it was daytime.

Bill had a suggestion. Why not dig around the top side of the end plate, and let the backhoe bucket hang one of the teeth under the plate and raise it up, so they can possibly prop it up.

They all thought that was a good idea, and a trench was dug, along the top of the plate away from the backhoe, and the operator extended the bucket, lowered it, and Bill guided it, until it was down, and behind the top of the plate.

He signaled to the operator to slowly raise the bucket, and the arm and the bucket came up slowly. The plate of steel, at first refused to move, but the operator increased the speed of the motor, and the plate moved slowly upwards.

When it was almost perpendicular, Bill signaled for the operator to stop. Two of the men, jumped into the hole and quickly propped the huge steel plate up and made sure it was fast, and would not fall.

Bill was disappointed, because under the plate was nothing but sand, however on the side next to the next plat, it looked as if there was an opening under the next plate.

They moved the backhoe over and repeated the same operation and sure enough there was a whole room beneath the steel plate. It had wooden stairs leading down into a large room as far as Bill could see for now.

There was no way to prop this plate up safely, so Bill asked the operator to just pull it on back to the opposite side of the hole.

He ordered everyone out of the hole and signaled the operator to go ahead and he did. The plate eased over and soon fell with a loud 'ploof' as it hit the ground!

The Lieutenant yelled for someone to bring the extension lights, as he and Bill was anxious to see what was in the room.

The lights were brought, and they looked down into the room, and were amazed at what they saw. There were wooden steps leading into the room, and in the room, were several large, locked boxes, all stacked on top of one another. All along the walls, there were oil lamps, and or candles placed so as to provide enough light.

They examined the steps for dry rot and to see if they might be able to go down them without breaking through the steps. They decided, they were in fairly good shape, good enough to hold them as they went down. At least, they hoped so!

Bill went first, slowly, very slowly, and was expecting to fall through at any moment, but he finally reached the ground, and he turned at told the Lieutenant, "Come on down, there's nothing to it."

The Lieutenant said, "Yeah, I seen just how there's nothing to it pace you were taking!"

Bill laughed and said, "I didn't think it showed that much!"

Finally, the Lieutenant reached the bottom also, and they looked around and they focused on the stacked large boxes. Bill reached up and brought one down so that they could further examine it.

It had a very large lock, through a large hasp, and Bill, started looking around for a bar of some kind to break it.

The Lieutenant yelled up and told them to bring them a crow bar and within a few moments, Bill was forcing the lock, and hasp. The lock, even though it was probably over a hundred or so years old, was very hard to break. But Bill was persistent, and soon, it gave and they raised the lid, and their eyes could not believe what they saw.

Bill reached in and pulled out a neatly wrapped pack of unused money. It was in 50 dollar bills and other packs were in 100 dollar bills. It was a fortune, and they had discovered it.

They looked at each other, laughed, and then Mary Jo came down the stairs, and asked, "What's all the laughter for?"

Bill didn't answer her, just pointed to the open crate, which she immediately looked into and she laughed a little, but then said, "Oh my goodness, a fortune, but it was only good in the years of 1861 to 1865! This is pure Confederate money!"

The crates were opened, one by one and they all contained the same thing. Neatly stacked

Confederate States money, not good for anything
at all!

The money was loaded, and carried to Bill's
office, and the A.B.I. team headed back to
Montgomery, after Bill personally thanked them
all. It was not a total loss, as they had the skull and
bones to examine and report on.

CHAPTER 17

The next morning, Bill called the newspapers,
radio and television stations in Montgomery and
Birmingham, and they all sent reporters for a news
conference he was holding about the discovery,
tomorrow, at 11:00 A.M.

The news conference was held in the meeting room of the City Council, and he invited the Mayor and members of the City council to be present if they so desired.

When 11:00 A.M. came, he was surprised at the television cameras, and microphones, and reporters that were in attendance for the news conference.

He was a little nervous staring into so many television cameras, he stumbled just a little at the start, but soon, he got over it and told the story of how and why he discovered the hidden money.

He thanked the Mayor, the City Council and of course, the Alabama Bureau of Investigation for all of their help, and without that, he could not have solved this part of the investigation.

When he opened the conference, one of the first questions asked was, "What did you mean, when you said this part of the investigation?"

Bill thought for a moment, and said slowly, "That part was meant for a certain individual or individuals, that know that I know they have something that I want set free, as it is now useless to keep this something. Now, with that said, I will not comment any more on that."

Another reporter asked, "How does it feel to hold $2,500,000 in your hands at one time, even if it was Confederate money?"

"Speaking for all my ancestors who fought for the South, it felt real good."

Still another question was, "What about the two skulls that you uncovered, that had holes in them?"

Bill answered as truthful as he could, "For the record, the Alabama Bureau of Investigation is still examining the two skulls, but preliminary results are maybe that they are two unlucky men that possibly dug the hole for the deposit of the money, and the crook or crooks wanted to hide their secret place!"

After the press conference, he went up to the café to eat with Mary Jo, and Marjorie. Pete, Marjorie's husband was there and was helping them as much as he could.

Mary Jo came over, and took his order, then asked, "How did the news conference go?"

Bill laughed, "I was nervous, but other than that, I think I did not make a fool out of myself."

Mary Jo patted him on the back and said, "You surely did not. We watched it live here on the television. You'd be surprised how many folks that were in here, and clapped for you. Man, you were a star!"

Bill blushed, "I'm certainly glad that's over. Say, where is Larry?"

"I don't know," she said, "just about the time you finished the news conference, he got a telephone call, turned a little pale, and without a word, just took off."

Bill stood up, and told Mary Jo to hold hid lunch, he'd be right back, and he hurried out the door.

When he pulled up to the apartment parking
lot, he looked but did not see Larry's pickup truck
anywhere, He went to Larry's apartment, listened,
and heard no sound, then knocked, but got no
response. He then walked to the manager's office
and told the lady, that it was necessary to enter
Larry's apartment. She refused at first, but Bill
explained that he was probably already gone, and
that he was part of a police investigation. She
immediately jumped up, grabbed the apartment
key from a hanger on the wall, and then let him in
the front room.

They both looked around, and all of his clothes
and anything else that belonged to him, was gone.
The apartment was empty, and the key was lying

on the desk. Apparently, he had made a quick departure!

Bill went back to the restaurant, ate his lunch, and was fixing to leave, when Marjorie came out of the kitchen, waving for Bill to wait.

She said that she had just found the keys to the restaurant, and any information that was needed to open and operate the business. Bill asked her if she and Pete could do it for a while longer.

Marjorie and Pete both answered yes, and Bill thanked them, said good bye to Mary Jo, and said, he would see her at 2:00 P.M.

When he got back to his office, he had a note to call his good friend in the Alabama Bureau of Investigation when he returned.

He called, and the gruff voice answered and said, "Son, that was a pretty dog-gone good press conference!"

"Why, thank you sir," answered Bill, "I hope that my message got through to the right people and results will soon begin to happen."

"Well," gruff voice said, "they already have. We have finally put two and two together and found who we think is Mr. Big. He's John Billington and his office is in the top of the tallest building in Birmingham."

"I'm going to get a warrant for his arrest and go get him," Bill said happily, "and just bring him down from that ivory tower!"

"What kind of a warrant," asked gruff voice.

"Kidnapping, "said Bill.

"You can't do it,' he said, "in the first place, you don't have enough evidence that he personally did the deed, and in the second place, you cannot find anyone that will swear that he even ordered it."

"You know," said Bill, dejectedly, "I know you're right, but I sure wanted to be the one to put handcuffs on him you know?"

"The Federal Bureau of Investigation is doing a little snooping around up there, so just keep your cool for a while, okay?"

"Okay, and say, thanks for all you help. I couldn't have done it without your assistance, and you have lost your youngest daughter you know. I'm going to ask her to marry me if that's okay with you!"

"Son, I couldn't select a better man for her. All I want from you is just to love and take care of her," he said, and Bill thought he was almost crying.

"That's one worry you don't have to have!"

CHAPTER 18

He and Mary Jo headed to Birmingham when she finished work, and they made it in about ninety minutes, and was soon parked outside the tallest building in Birmingham, the Billington Building.

They got out and walked across the street, and entered the sliding doors, and there was a big round desk in the middle of the room. Behind it was about six young women, each with a sign above their head that denoted the particular company or companies they represented.

There were six elevators and a security guard at each one. Each security guard looked as if they used to play in the national Football League, and nobody got past them without a pass issued by the ladies at the desk, or they had a permanent pass attached to their lapels.

Each elevator led to a different company, all owned by Billington. All of his enterprises were located in one building, at least, that was the idea and the impression he wanted to portray.

Bill and Mary Jo took a seat away from the action and sat down and discussed just how they might get upstairs to the very top office. They set and watched the flow of people in and out of the elevators, and Mary Jo suddenly got up, and walked over to an office guide, and studied the different companies listed there.

She came back and leaned over, and whispered to Bill, "The top most company is a printing concern, and they are on the very top floor, right below the penthouse office."

"Good work, honey," Bill said, "now let's find out which we have to talk too to get a pass to that floor."

They went up to the round desk, and soon were in front of the young receptionist, and asked for a pass to the printing company. The young lady looked quizzical, and asked, "Why do you want to go up there? Nobody ever wants to see those people."

Bill coughed and said, "We represent Acme Machinery Company, and we have a new line of printing equipment to show them."

"Well, from what I've heard, they sure could use some new equipment," she said as she writing and then stamped the two passes.

Bill and Mary Jo quickly attached the passes to their lapels, and walked up to the appropriate elevator and showed the guard their passes, and he opened the door for them. They punched the highest floor on the control panel, the doors closed and they were soon zipping up towards the top of the building.

When they arrived at the designated floor, a bell rung, and the doors opened. They saw a room full of copiers, and all types of printing presses. They slowly stepped off the elevator, and a young black woman walked by, and Bill stopped her and asked, "How do we get to the office of Mr. Billington?"

She looked at them for a moment, as if she was real busy, too busy to fool with them, but she finally said, "Oh, just follow me."

Mary Jo, followed by Bill fell in behind her as they twisted and turned and finally came to another elevator. Bill thanked her, and she walked off, and Mary Jo, pressed the button, and they heard the car coming.

When the door opened, they stepped in, and as soon as they did, the door shut, and it sped up until it reached what was apparently the floor of "Mr. Big."

Bill reached behind him and felt his snub-nosed .38 tucked safely in his waistband just as the door opened. They looked at the room before entering.

"Come in, Bill, Come in, you too Mary Jo," and Bill was sure he recognized the voice. It was very familiar.

He held Mary Jo back, and eased into the room, and there was a very large desk, sitting off to the right, and the familiar voice was attached to one, Timothy McDermott.

Bill had a look of surprise on his face and it must have showed, because again, Timothy said, "Come on in, you two. You're welcome. This is my office now, and you're quite welcome!"

They both eased in and Bill helped Mary Jo sit down in a chair in front of the desk, and he casually set in the other.

He said, "Honey, you have heard me talk of my good friend, Timothy McDermott, haven't you, well, this is he!"

"It is a pleasure to meet you, Mary Jo," Timothy said.

"It's a pleasure to meet you too," she replied.

Bill turned serious, the smile went off his face and he looked Timothy directly in the eyes and said, "Timothy, my friend, I've come to arrest you. You're "Mr. Big" and that's what I am here for."

Timothy laughed a little and said, "Bill, I'll tell you a little story, and at the end, if you're not convinced, I'll go with you, without any objections what so ever, is that a deal?"

Bill thought for a moment, then, asked, "All right Timothy, what have you got up your sleeve?"

"Nothing, nothing at all, but what I really want is for you to listen for a few minutes. Now is that too much to ask," he said.

"Okay, I'm all ears," said Bill, and he heard Mary Jo snigger when he said that, and he turned and stuck his tongue out at her.

Timothy started telling them what he wanted to say, "Bill, my grandfather passed away two weeks ago and he was known as "Mr. Big." And he was just that. There's something else you should know is, Mr. Walker Rogers of Rogersville, is my great-grandfather. That's something that I have found out in the last few days,"

"So," Bill interjected, "I'm sorry to hear about your grandfather, but he is the Mr. Billington, the missing son of Mr. Rogers. But, what is he doing in Alabama?"

"That's what I am coming too, so hold your horses. Rogers thought that they were in California somewhere, but never dreamed they were only about 90 miles away in Birmingham all the time."

Timothy got up from the desk and walked over to a hidden refrigerator, and opened it and took out three soft drinks, opened them, and handed one to Bill, and Mary Jo.

He sat on the edge of his desk, and continued, "Grandpa, made a little money, here. and there and h would always put it back into something else and pretty soon, it began to double, then triple. He then bought a coal mine, that some experts said was depleted of coal, but he knew better, and that's where he made his first million."

"Grandpa was a smart cookie when it came to investing, and know how and when to buy out certain companies, that he soon became known as 'Mr. Big' all over the state,"

"Why," asked Mary Jo, "if he had so much money, why did he want more and more?"

"Who really knows," said Timothy, "once you get the want of a million, then you want two, then four, then six and so on, I guess!"

"The love of money," she said sadly.

"Yes, the love of more money." he said, and when he found out that there was $2,500,000 missing from the steamboat, he figured it had to be hidden on the old Rogers Plantation, his ancestors place, but he was too late to buy all the property, only forty acres was left."

"So what you are telling us is that when we found the money, and it was all Confederate States paper money and not gold, he lost interest," Bill exclaimed.

"That's about it," said Timothy.

Bill slowly shook his head in disbelief, and then he turned to Timothy, and asked,

"Now, please tell me, what happened to the Roberts, Hales, the Suttons, Paul McAndrew and Matthew Grayson?"

Timothy laughed and said, "Not what you think, Bill. But, the Suttons, Hales, and Roberts should be back in Rogersville by now, enjoying their $50,000 check courtesy of the hotel, and while they were gone, they were not really kidnapped, they were guests of our company so to speak."

"Now, what in the blue blazes does that mean," Bill asked.

"It simply means that they enjoyed a trip to the Caribbean, all expenses paid, trip to South America, all expenses paid, all on board my Grandpa's 80 foot yacht!"

"But what about McAndrew and Grayson."

"Paul McAndrew," Timothy returned to his desk chair, "was my grandfather's personal valet for thirty years. He is now at his boyhood home in Scotland. He always talked about wanting to go home one day, so my grandfather located the home place, bought it in Paul's name, and give it to him, along with $2,000,000 to live on for the remainder of his life!"

"Wow," said Mary Jo, enthusiastically, "that was certainly a great present for many years of service."

"Now," Bill asked, "what about Matthew Grayson?"

Timothy looked at Bill, and smiled a little, and said, "Now, that's the key to the whole puzzle.

Matthew Grayson, as you knew him, was really my Grandfather, John Billington. He was living there in Rogersville, all the time, unknown, as he wanted it."

Bill sat back, hardly wanting to believe what he had just heard. Matthew Grayson, the mild mannered man, who was very nice and polite to everyone, was really one of the richest men in Alabama, if not the United States.

Then another question popped into his mind, "Timothy, what about the bum that was claiming to be Ricky Roberts nephew? What happened to him?"

Timothy smiled, and said, "We have offices and companies all over the world. And that includes the areas close to the North and South poles. So, guess where he is."

Bill and Mary Jo laughed along with Timothy, and then they got up to leave.

Timothy said, "Bill, things will be different now that I am in charge. No more undercover shenanigans, and such. I want us to be friends, and, by the way, that job is still open."

Bill said, "As far as I am concerned, I will always be you friend, unless you send a skunk to Rogersville like Larry, then we just might become unfriends, quick like, you know. I still cannot accept the job at this time, maybe later, but not right now."

Timothy looked at him, and said seriously, "Okay, but it's there if you want it, and don't worry, the 'skunk' mistake will never be made again." He stuck out his hand, and shook Bill's hand with a tight grip.

He hugged Mary Jo, and as they turned to wait for the elevator door to open, Timothy said, "If you two don't send me an invite to the wedding, I'll just up and cry like a baby!"

Mary Jo hugged his neck and said, "I'll see that you get one, if I have to hand deliver it!"

The bell rang, the door opened, and they boarded the car, and the door shut behind them, the first step on their way back to the little, peaceful town of Rogersville.

THE END